Falling for the Fake Boyfriend

Clearview Falls University Book #1

S.E. Rose

Sierra Hill

Chapter One

E mmett

"Emmett, honey? Is that you?"

I step over the threshold of the back door leading into the kitchen where it's nearly dark, the only light coming faintly from the living room around the corner. The scent of cinnamon sticks and cloves immediately hits my nostrils and sends a flood of emotion to my brain.

"Yeah, it's me, Nana. Sorry I'm late, practice ran over today. But I have the groceries and your meds."

I flip on the overhead light in the small and warm kitchen, setting down the bag of groceries I picked up on my way over from football practice.

One look at the unkempt kitchen—the unwashed plates piling up in the sink, and the greasy mucky gunk stuck at the bottom of the roast pan from Sunday's dinner—and guilt washes over me.

It's been a bad week for her, and I should've made time to visit sooner than today.

"Fuck," I mutter to myself. It's going to be a long night ahead of me. This situation is getting worse, nearly unmanageable for me to keep up with everything I have on my plate, and I'm at a loss of what to do. I fear I won't be able to keep up anymore.

It's not going to be my college education or my spot on the Clearview Falls U football team, that's for sure. I will do anything for my grandmother but when push comes to shove, I'll find another solution before I drop out of school or lose my hard-won position as the team's wide receiver.

The fridge is practically empty when I open it up to put away the perishables I bought at the market in town. There's a leftover casserole that one of Nana's church friends brought over earlier in the week that looks like it's done for, some wilted salad mix, and a half-eaten apple.

Nana hasn't been eating much lately. She claims she's watching her girlish figure, but I know it's more than that. At seventy-two, she has been plagued by a plethora of medical ailments over the past five years but most notably her MS, which has progressively worsened, leaving her in considerable pain and a reduction in mobility.

I drive her to her monthly treatments, but the flare-ups of chronic muscular pain and temporary paralysis have become so frequent that they impair her ability to move around on her own and her quality of life, leaving her alone and in a wheelchair.

It sucks because Nana is the only person left in my life I can count on. It's definitely not my dad, who has proven time and time again that he's only out for his own best interests. Case in point, I'm here and he's not.

"Honey, come on in and sit for a spell. The groceries

can wait. I want to catch up with you. Tell me how your week is going."

I finish with the remaining pantry items and grab two waters, then round the corner into the living room where the sight of my grandma gives me a stabbing pain in my heart. It's only been four days since I last visited, but I swear she looks smaller and more frail each time I see her.

It makes me sad and angry all at once. Thank God I can take it out on the football grid; otherwise, I might just break down and sob. Or break things. But I know that won't help.

Despite her issues, Nana's smile remains big and proud and gives me an instant dose of happiness.

"There's my boy!" She opens her arms wide, like she's parting the Red Sea from her chair. "Come over here and give your old Nana a hug."

I do as she says and place the bottles down on her TV tray next to her overstuffed lounger, then gently wrap her body into my arms. I'm always careful not to embrace her too tightly for fear of unintentionally breaking a bone or squeezing her airways closed.

She gives me a light peck on the cheek and I stand back to move some papers from the chair next to her so I can sit down.

I notice that most of them look like credit card statements and doctor bills, a reminder that I need to go through her finances next week and send off her monthly payments.

Ruth Nadine Jackson Hudson is my dad's mother. My middle name is Jackson, after her maiden name. The dad who for all intents and purposes is dead to me. The guy who siphoned money from his own parents' accounts after my granddad's death and used it in some Ponzi scheme to get rich.

When that didn't work, he took off to avoid the law and

legal prosecution, leaving me to hold down the fort when I was fifteen.

My grandma never talks about Dad's mess with me. But I know she still loves her son, despite how he's used her. I'd bet dollar to dollar that if he called her up asking for help, she'd give all she could.

That's the kind of woman she is and the reason I'm here. To protect the one I love and care for her like she did for me all these years.

We're all that we have left in this world and she's the only one who's stuck by my side. I've tried to do the same for her, even though I feel guilty as hell I'm not doing more. I could have dropped out of school and found a full-time job to help with her financial situation but she wouldn't hear of it. Wouldn't listen to reason. She keeps saying it isn't my burden to take on and I have to live my own life, which in her book means finishing school and playing football.

I've done what she's asked but I don't feel good about it. Which is why I took on a part-time job off campus at the hardware store to help pay for necessities. It's not much and doesn't leave me much time for parties or social events, or even a girlfriend, but it's what I need to do.

You take care of the ones you love and protect them at all costs. No matter the personal costs. My asshat dad certainly didn't teach me this important life lesson but that doesn't mean I don't know it because Nana instilled that moral in me.

Nana pats my knee in that gentle prodding gesture of hers. "How did practice go today? Are you all ready for the big game on Saturday?"

I glance at the time on my phone before silencing it and shoving it in my pocket. It's after five right now and I still have dinner to make, some bills to pay, and laundry to do before I head back to the house I share with my friends. Then I have to book it to the library where I have my first required tutoring session tonight.

Oh, yeah. That's another thing forced upon me that I don't have time for but have no other option but to do.

I inhale deeply and let out a big sigh. Then I dutifully begin telling my grandmother all the details about my week.

It'll be a long night but I'm not going to rush my time with Nana. There's nothing more important than her.

* * *

It's just past eight thirty when I get back to my off-campus house and walk upstairs to the room I share with Killian, where I immediately notice Killer's game-day tie hanging from the doorknob.

Great. Thanks a lot, bro.

Killian Palmer, aka Killer, is my best friend, teammate, and roommate. We were paired up as incoming freshmen due to the football roster and our positions on the team, and have ended up practically inseparable for the past 3 years.

Except on occasions like this, when he brings some chick back to the room to smash.

I yank the tie from the knob and grumble. We'd made a pact earlier this semester that no girls were allowed over on weeknights. Despite my momentary irritation, it's not the worst thing in the world. I just need to grab my backpack and laptop from my desk before I head to the library for my nine o'clock appointment with my tutor.

I shoot Killer a quick text, hoping they are almost done and I can just sneak in and grab my things.

Me: Yo. I need my bag, bro. Can I come in and get it?

I notice the three dots appearing on my screen and hear his loud clomping footsteps across the floor, then the door swings open. There before me stands my ginger-blond roommate, hair rumpled, feet and chest bare, and hand covering his junk.

Smirking, he holds out the backpack toward me.

"Give me till midnight," he requests as I snag the bag from his fingers. Without waiting for an answer, he shuts the door in my face. I hear his loud stomping feet again, presumably toward his bed, then a girlish giggle and a yelp of laughter.

"Glad one of us is getting some."

It's not like I feel sorry for myself. Okay, maybe a little. I haven't been with a girl since this summer, before school started up again. And it doesn't look promising with the commitments I already have in my life.

All I know is that, after the conversation Coach had with me this afternoon after practice, the details of which I conveniently left out from my conversation with Nana earlier, I don't have any room for even casual hookups right now. Coach had sat me down, said he received our mid-semester grade reports from the Admin office, and proceeded to assign me with a tutor.

Perfect. Now on top of everything else on my plate I need to find time to squeeze two to three hours a week of tutoring into my schedule.

But if I don't get my grades up—especially in Microbiology, which I'm on my way to failing—I can kiss both the field and my scholarships for next year goodbye.

I roll my eyes at the prospect as I leave the house and

head out down the block to the library. I try to keep my head low, my baseball cap pulled down over my eyes so when I pass friends and acquaintances along the way, I won't be noticed. They'll want to stop and chat and I don't have the time.

The only problem with this covert operation is that I don't see the oncoming person soon enough to move out of the way.

What a shit-tastic way to end my night.

Chapter Two

L ucy

I roll the pen's cap back and forth over my lower lip as I study the assigned reading for my organic chemistry class. This is the class that everyone in my major talks about with disdain, but I love it.

What I don't love is being stood up for my first tutoring session by this guy.

I glance at the library clock on the wall and let out a disgruntled groan. I never should have scheduled a late-night tutoring session with some jock, but it was a last-minute request and I needed the extra money, so I took the job.

Now I'm regretting that choice. I start to pack up my things from my study cube, angrily stuffing my books into my backpack and making enough noise to alert someone of my presence back here.

But the likelihood of that is slim; not many people venture back into this hidden area. Last year, a librarian I'd become friendly with showed me this spot behind old periodical shelves on the top floor of the library. If you peer around them, it just looks like some old desks piled up, but if you manage to scoot behind, you find yourself in a small enclave with four built-in desks, a remnant of the library before it was remodeled.

It's perfect for tutoring sessions because it's quiet and nobody disturbs us.

Considering the location, I suppose there's always a chance that my new student may be lost, but I always provide expert directions.

Still, I consider this possibility as I work my way through the periodicals, on my way down to the main floor, and feel my phone buzz in my pocket. I pull it out and see a text notification from my older brother, Landon. He's a firefighter back in our hometown of Rivers Crossing, which is a whopping forty-five minutes away from school. I wanted some freedom when I chose a college, but also to be close enough for family visits.

> Landon: Hope your test goes well this week! Maybe I'll stop by in a few weeks when I'm out your way to pick up some new special-ordered helmets.

I smile. My big brother is the best. Always has been.

> Me: Sounds good. And thanks.

Landon was one of the key reasons I chose to study at Clearview Falls University. That, and the amazing microbiology program. Plus, CFU gave me the best scholarship offer, so here I am.

My brother likes to tease me, calling me a homebody because, other than going to classes and hanging with my besties Gracie and Kelsie, I'm not very involved at school. I'm not much for parties—unless I'm dragged to them, kicking and screaming, by the girls—or any of the other on-campus social events.

And team sports? Not in a million years. The noise levels alone produce an overwhelming feeling of being trapped. Not my thing. Not to say I don't admire the talents of athletes or their dedication to their chosen sport, I just can't deal with crowds or screaming.

But when my favorite professor from freshman year asked me to join his tutoring program, I begrudgingly said yes. At the very least, it looks good on my resume and gives me extra spending money.

Of course, the one student I make an exception for and take on at the last minute is some dumb football player who clearly doesn't know how to tell time or respect someone else's time. I cringe at my bad luck, hefting up the pile of books in my hands to readjust so I can press the elevator button.

It just goes to show that I'm invisible to the football players. Always have been, especially the one I've had a huge crush on since high school. Joel Henderson would probably walk right by me on campus and totally not know who I am.

Ugh! I feel my face heat just thinking about him. He was the captain of our high school football team and every girl's secret crush. I hated myself for liking him. I was just the nerdy science girl with the glasses in the class below him.

While he broke school records and girls' hearts throughout high school, I was president of the Science Club, treasurer of the Math Club, and one of the set builders for the class plays and school musicals.

Although not many boys noticed me, I still noticed them. They still had an effect on me. I wasn't particularly shy or introverted, just anxious around too many people, and I've even been told I'm kind of pretty.

But unfortunately, I get anxious around too many people, and I felt more comfortable hiding my attributes under big bulky hoodies.

I even dated a guy from the drama club for six months my junior year, but then his dad's work relocated them to Florida and we broke up. Landon keeps telling me to let loose and live a little, enjoy my college years. He's not wrong, but my social anxiety is still my worst enemy. It's why I like my safe space in the back of the library where people can't see me and vice versa.

Maybe that's why this dumb jock didn't show up. Oh well, his tough luck.

Reaching the front entrance, I check my watch again and grow more inpatient and anxious by the second as I glance down over the stack of books in my hand. In the emails we exchanged prior to this meet-up, I'd told him exactly where to meet me and stressed the time. My intent was clear. *Be on time and don't waste my time.*

Yet here I am, waiting for him to arrive, me on schedule and him nowhere to be found.

I tap my foot and, at ten minutes after the hour, I give up. Is he being intentionally rude and disrespectful, or did something happen?

Giving him the benefit of the doubt, I open up the last

message exchange, thinking maybe he messaged me that he was running late. Nope. Nothing. Just his last text:

See you at nine.

Feeling stupidly angry and oddly rejected, I practically sprint out of the library in my haste to get back to my dorm room. I hate walking alone at night. Although there's plenty of light along the walkways to the dorms, and the campus is small and safe, my brother has instilled in me the need to always be cautious of my surroundings, especially when by myself.

I jog down four steps, careful not to lose my balance or the grip I have on my books, and keep my gaze plastered to my feet to avoid tripping.

And then, in the next instant, I'm colliding straight into a wall of human.

"Whoa!" A guy's deep voice surrounds me and large solid hands clasp around my arms.

My books crash to the ground and scatter at my feet, but I'm saved from following them by whoever is currently holding me upright. I lurch forward, my hands flailing and seeking purchase with the first thing I can find—*ooof*.

Holy shit, this guy's muscles are hard as bricks. My brain tells me to let go, but something else inside me refuses to listen.

"You okay?" he asks. I slowly lift my head and stare straight into two dark eyes surrounded by the type of lashes girls pay good money to have. I recognize him because he's always around Joel Henderson—or Hendy, as everyone calls him—and the other crew of impossibly large football play-ers. but I don't know his name. Is this the guy I'm supposed to be tutoring?

I swallow down my embarrassment and slowly pull away. He immediately kneels down and begins to pick up my books, one by one, as a few people leaving the library slow down to see what's going on. Probably curious—with phones at the ready, no doubt—to film what happened or why he's helping me out.

"Emmett?" My voice sounds hesitant as I too bend over to assist in the collection of my strewn books.

Our gazes lock and all the anxiety I had earlier now turns into butterflies in the pit of my stomach. Our faces are so close I can see a scar on the left side of his eye that looks like a crescent moon.

Feeling my cheeks heat with the proximity of our bodies, I quickly stand and take a step back, adjusting the books I've now collected in my hands. As he rises, the muscle in his jaw clenches tightly and then releases.

"Hey, yeah. Are you Lucy?" he asks quietly, his eyes darting around us, assessing our surroundings. Is he embarrassed to be seen with me?

Sighing, I nod. "Yep. And you're ten minutes late," I note, scanning him up and down with a scolding look. "You've missed your tutoring session and I'm going to leave."

His baseball cap sits low on his head and a CFU Bears hoodie disguises his built body, as if he's trying to be an undercover spy. I shake my head. Typical. Probably afraid to be seen at a library.

"Uh, yeah. Sorry about that," he mutters, removing the hat and sliding a hand through his light brown hair. "I didn't mean to be late."

I scoff, my voice laced with annoyance. "Whatever. It doesn't matter because you're late and that cuts into my life. For future reference, please try to be on time from here out.

I'm sure you're used to being catered to, but I can't wait around for you just because of who you are."

"Right. Of course."

While he doesn't outright glare at me, his mouth pinches and his facial expression clearly reads he's not happy about having to be here or in my presence.

Well, that makes two of us.

I roll my eyes. I should just leave his ass here, but my too polite and bending need to be liked tells me otherwise.

"Fine, come on. We can get in at least 30 minutes." I turn around and trudge back up the stairs, glancing at him over my shoulder when we reach the doors. "I can take the books." I motion to my books he still carries in his hands.

He looks me up and down. "They won't fit in that giant bag of yours?"

I bite my lip because my bag is actually filled with lab samples that I collected for an independent research project. I shake my head.

"It's cool. I can just carry them," he says, tucking them in the crook of his arm like he would a football before opening the door with his free hand. I stare at his giant bear paw and marvel at its size. This guy is massive and the exact opposite of microbiology. Everything about him is big, ginormous even.

I walk inside at a clipped pace as he follows behind me. I wind around the shelves of books and periodicals and lead him upstairs to my secret study spot. He sets my books down and stares at me expectantly as he plops down at the table and I take the seat next to him.

"So...like, what can you help me with?" he asks, extracting his laptop from his backpack, which is also emblazoned with the Bears logo. Talk about school spirit. I wonder if I even own anything with that graphic outside of a gray hoodie I bought freshman year.

"You're in Professor Watkins' class, right?" I ask.

He nods and clicks a few buttons, opening up his class portal page.

"I took it last year with him. What section are you currently working on?" I ask, leaning over to get a good look at the webpage. He points.

"Just to get a baseline for where you stand, are you familiar with biology? Did you take it in high school?"

He shrugs. "Yeah. Something like that."

I want so badly to roll my eyes but keep myself in check. I know from firsthand experience when I was in high school that the teachers often allowed student athletes to skate by in order to remain on the school sport teams.

"Let me guess. This wasn't your idea to get tutoring, was it?" I pin him with a look. "You're here because you need a passing grade to stay on the team. Right?"

His eyes dart from the computer screen to my face. For a microsecond, I swear a look of hurt passes over his face, but it quickly turns into an icy glare.

"I don't need your patronizing comments or questions. All I need is your help. Are you going to give it to me or not? I don't have time to waste, either," he growls.

"Fine. But here are my rules." I lean forward in the chair, plunking my elbow on the table and counting off my expectations one by one with my fingers. "One, you are on time. Two, you stay for the full hour. Three, if I give you something to read or learn, you study it and you do it. Comprendé?"

I'm nearly shaking inside because I've never been this sure about myself before. I have no idea where this is coming from or why. Normally I'd tuck tail and run and hide.

He shakes his head and drops his head back between his shoulders, his eyes staring up to the ceiling for a moment before returning his attention to me. "Yes," he grits out, his teeth clenched.

"Cool. Then, let's begin here." I pull out my laptop. "I have your email, so I'll just send you this outline I made for the class. It's pretty basic, but it should cover everything. Let's spend tonight going over the lessons you've covered in class so far this semester. I just want to make sure you understand the basics." Like, one plus one is two and the sky is blue.

God, what have I gotten myself into with this guy?

"Well, don't beat around the bush," he mumbles.

"I don't plan on it. I'm not going to coddle you because you're a prized football player. That would be a severe disservice to everyone and a waste of both our valuable time."

We glare at each other like two opponents on the field. Little does he know. I might think football players are notoriously dumb and arrogant based on my experiences with them.

I turn my screen toward him. "Shall we begin?"

He takes a breath and nods. I watch as he pulls out an oversized water bottle and takes a gulp, his throat muscles working fast. It sends a strange zing down my spine. I might be frustrated with how things have started out with him, but there's no denying he's very attractive.

For one, he's the biggest guy I've ever seen or been next to. His body takes up a vast amount of space. My guess is he's probably close to six feet two and must weigh over 200 pounds, at least. I'm an average-size girl, but next to him I feel petite.

I continue staring as he removes his ball cap, shrugs off his sweatshirt, then slips the hat back on, this time backwards. He settles into his chair, his arm muscles bulging from his short-sleeved T-shirt.

From the side, I notice that his cheeks are rosy, like he's either just finished a workout or he ran here and is overly heated from the strenuous nature of the exercise. The slope of his nose is proportionate to his face and he has a faint dusting of freckles at the bridge of his nose. There is a lingering bit of scruff across his jaw that's a little darker than the hair peeking out from underneath his ball cap.

I have a strange magnetic need to stare at his facial features a while longer, but right now it's more important to finish up this tutoring lesson and get the hell back to my dorm. And away from the alarming appeal of Emmett Hudson.

I shake away my thoughts. Thank God I'll only have to deal with him for six more weeks. Six weeks of giving this gorgeous ogre lessons. Then I can add the required tutoring sessions to my resume and maybe convince Professor Watkins to let me take his graduate level class next year, even though I'll only be a junior.

As for Emmett, I just hope he takes this seriously and doesn't make my life a living hell. Because there is no way I'm putting up with any shit from this guy, no matter how hot he is.

Chapter Three

E mmett

What stick does this chick have up her butt? And what the hell did I do to make her immediately dislike me?

I'm a pretty likable guy. At least that's what my friends and teachers have always said. I'm chill, easygoing. Reliable. I look after those I care about, I don't intentionally piss people off for no reason.

So why has Lucy decided upon making me out to be a villain in this story?

It's these thoughts that keep me awake most of the night. Why do I even care what she thinks? I sat at the kitchen table and finished up my paper for my communication class while waiting until Killer escorted his hookup out of the room. Looking all smug and shit, I might add.

After that, we stayed up for another hour playing a

video game and talking about the upcoming Saturday game against the Titans.

"Have you seen that Miller guy since last season?" Killian asks, his thumbs moving rapid-fire over his controller. "The dude has to be jacked up and juicing some 'roids or something. He gained at least fifty pounds since last season."

I lift a shoulder. "I don't know. That's making a big assumption. I mean, look at you, bro. You put on some serious muscle this summer, too."

Killian pauses the game and turns with a grin, showing off his guns with the flex of his biceps before kissing both bulges like a goddamn idiot. "This, my friend, is 100% all natural Iowa-bred man meat. And the ladies love it."

I give him an eye roll, tossing the controller to the side in favor of shoving him in the chest so he falls sideways like a giant sack of potatoes. Killer barks out a laugh.

"You're fucking full of yourself, bro."

"Meh, it's working for me. I mean, look at that chick I boned tonight. I wouldn't have had a chance in hell with her last year. But now? I've got it going on."

He stands up and struts around the room like he's Arnold Schwarzenegger during his bodybuilding days. I'll admit, Killer definitely added some muscle mass since the end of last school year. He's not hefty or bulky like a linebacker, and isn't as big as NFL tight ends like Rob Gronkowski or Kyle Rudolphs, but he's definitely packing it on this year.

I maneuver onto my bed, shifting the books and laptop over so I have room to stretch out. Rolling to my side, I prop my head up with my palm, knowing if my head lands on that pillow, it's lights out for me.

"What's your secret then?"

Killian stops his catwalk and looks at me. "Secret for what? The chicks or my form?"

I laugh when he waggles his eyebrows in a suggestive manner. If there's one thing to say about my roommate, it's that he's a goof. Never takes himself or life too seriously. He loves football, animals, his younger sisters, and his parents' farm back in Iowa, and he knows he's going to run the family business after he graduates with a degree in agricultural studies. I wish I had the same level of confidence in my future career aspirations as he does.

"Both, I suppose. Because I hardly have time for the bare minimum between football practice, games, workouts, studying, and checking in on my Nana. And now I have to work with this lame-ass tutor who hates my guts."

Killian pulls out his desk chair and straddles it backwards, leaning over the backrest with his elbows pointed outwards.

"Yeah, what's up with that, man? Coach Brewster seriously gave you an ultimatum?"

I scowl. "Yep. Said I'd be benched if I didn't get my grades up. I mean, I *am* pretty close to failing my lab science class. Which is why I have to meet with this stick-up-her-butt tutor named Lucy."

Killian grabs the T-shirt hanging over the side of his chair and whips it at me.

"Bro, I could've helped you out there. You know I'm a motherfucking genius when it comes to the sciences."

"Nah, bruh. You have enough on your plate as it is." I shake my head then drop it to my pillow. "Plus, I'd hate to eat into your hookup time."

He gives me a cheesy grin. "Good point. The ladies are lining up for the Killer D."

Killian makes a lewd gesture toward his crotch and I close my eyes but smile over his antics.

It's what I like most about Killian. He's a big talker Betty Crocker but has a heart of gold. He's the best friend I could have, one I know will always have my back, whether out on the field or in real life.

"How about you and your supposed Big D shutting the fuck up now so I can get some sleep?"

* * *

The morning team workout session is brutal. Even Killian is sweating it out as our athletic trainers and coaches push us hard toward eventual collapse or tossing up our breakfasts. It's all to up the ante as we get closer to the end-of-the-season championships.

This year we are tied with our rivals, the Grand Junction Titans, who we face off with this coming Saturday. Luckily, it's a home game and ,with the ravenous football fans in the school and the community, we should have a fucking fantastic game.

I lay with my back on the bench press, getting a spot from Killian, when Joel "Hendy" Henderson, our team's quarterback this year, comes striding by, clutching a towel wrapped around his neck.

"Hey, guys. How are my two favorite offensive players doing?"

Hendy snaps Killian in the gut with his towel before he squats down next to me and eyes the weight rack.

With Killian's help, we stack the weight bar back in the cradle and I sit upright, legs straddling the bench, and wipe the sweat dripping down my arms with my own towel. Hendy hands me my water bottle sitting at my feet.

"Thanks, man. We're good. How about you?"

I didn't know Hendy very well last year when he was still second-string, but now that he's moved up after last year's starting quarterback graduated and we've had more playing time together, we've become better friends. In fact, so much so that we're all sharing a house this year.

He's a good guy, a little arrogant around some people, but decent enough to me and Killian. And now that he's starting QB, he gets more pussy than any other guy on this campus. I wonder how many times a month he has to get tested for STIs?

I drop my chin down to hide the laughter threatening to pop free from my chest as Killian starts chatting with Hendy.

"You ready for Saturday's game?"

Hendy gives him a *what do you think, bro* side eye. "Dude, I was born ready. We're going to crush the Titans. They don't stand a chance." Hendy points an index finger first at Killian and then at me with a pointed look. "As long as I get the coverage from my offensive line and my passes are caught by my receivers. You feel me, EJ? Killer?"

We both nod dutifully, Killian thumping Hendy on the shoulder.

"We got you, bro."

Seemingly satisfied with this response, Hendy smiles and gives us both fist bumps. "That's what I'm talking about. Teamwork and tenacity." He quotes Coach Brewster's motto like the good soldier he is. "And after we win on Saturday night, it's gonna be lit at the Delta Kappa house. You both going?"

Hendy is a member of the frat, even though he lives in an-off Greek row house with us. I glance up at Killian who grins wildly. "Hell yeah, we're going. It's our duty to take care of our female fans who want the winning Ds."

Hendy laughs, slapping Killian across the back. I shake my head and take another drink from my water bottle.

"Damn straight, boys," Hendy chuckles. "It's our duty to score on the field and in the frat houses."

That's Hendy for you.

I guess I can't blame the guy. I'd probably be the same if I were in his shoes. He has girls surrounding him day and night wanting a piece of him. I've never heard anything negative or creepy about his behavior, which is good, because I'd not think twice about turning in a douchewad who isn't respectful of other humans. But he sure does go through girls faster than I do clean T-shirts in a week.

"Carry on, Killer. EJ. I'll see you guys later."

Hendy thumps us both on the back before he heads off toward the physio room to get work done on his shoulder by our team therapist.

Killian watches him walk off, a look of awe crossing his face.

"What I wouldn't give for a day in his life," he says dreamily.

I sniff. "I don't know, man. That's a lot of pressure on his shoulders. He's the face of the team and if he fucks up or the team does, he's the one who gets the shaft. I wouldn't want that."

I stand up and stretch out my arms and shoulders, then move around to the back of the bench, allowing Killian to take my place.

"You're up, bro. Let's see if you can put your muscles where your mouth is."

Chapter Four

L ucy

"You can't wear that," Kelsie states, duly mortified at my ensemble.

I purse my lips and glare at her. "What's wrong with a hoodie? It's cold and we are going to an outdoor football game." I've barely gotten the sentence out of my mouth when Kelsie throws open the door to my pathetically small closet and begins ransacking it, tossing various articles of clothing on my bed.

"We are going to the Delta Kappa party *after* the game. We don't have time to change. You need to layer," she huffs as she holds up a tank top and cocks her head to the side.

"I have a T-shirt on under this. That's layering," I state with a sarcastic lilt, lifting the hem of the sweatshirt to prove my point.

"Yeah, and that T-shirt is like two sizes too large." She waves her hand. "Is it your brother's?"

I look down at the front of my T-shirt and realize she might be right.

Gracie steps out of the bathroom just then and gives a little spin. Gracie is adorable with a capital A. Tiny with sleek black hair that she has twirled up into two buns at the top of her head and dark eyes lined with an onyx liner and long inky-colored lashes. Tonight she has on jeans, a crop top in our school colors, and cowboy boots.

"You're gonna be cold," I point out dutifully, sounding like a parent and not a friend.

She reaches into her strapless bra and pulls out something that resembles one of those fake boob things that girls wear to make them look more well-endowed. Only, it has a little screw top on the side of it.

"No, I won't. And neither will you." She winks, her eyelashes fluttering expressively. "Look at this flask my cousin sent me. It's legit OG!" Gracie squeals as she opens the silver lid and takes a sip. "Here, we can start tailgating now."

I groan as Kelsie opens my desk drawer and pulls out scissors. Before I can even speak, she's cutting off half of my tank top.

"What the hell are you doing?"

"Improvising. We need to update your wardrobe," she says as she continues to mutilate my shirt. I grab for it and she turns so I can't reach it.

"Kels! What the hell?" I yell, scrambling to gather clothing she's determined to destroy. Unlike her and Grace, I don't have the extra money to put towards a new wardrobe. They both come from wealthy families and are able to buy everything they need and want.

"There," she announces proudly as she holds it up to survey her work before tossing it at me. "Put that on. Let's see."

My roommates both sit down on my bed, waiting expectantly for me to change. I grumble and yank off my hoodie and T-shirt.

"Ew, no. That bra will not do," Kelsie exclaims, brushing past me to her bureau to open the top drawer. "Use this. Cause I know you don't have anything beyond that mom bra."

"Why do I feel judged?" I ask myself out loud, taking it from her extended hand and examining it like I would a rabid animal, as if it might strike and bite me at any moment.

"We aren't judging, Lucy, we're helping," Gracie says proudly, her speech already a little slurred. Then she juts out her hip and shimmies her shoulders. "Plus, Hendy will be there."

I groan again as I turn to put on the bra, squishing my C-sized breasts into her barely B-cups. Since Gracie has been my best friend since 7th grade, she knows all about my super-secret crush on Joel, who is a year ahead of us. Kelsie is the only other person that knows about my long-time attraction to the guy.

Sadly, I'm not sure he even knows who I am or that we went to the same high school. And I doubt that will ever change. He's so far out of my league he practically lives on a different planet than me. I'm still just some nerdy nobody to him, and one of the many girls who never stand a chance with him.

I put on the now very short tank top and turn around, covering my midriff with my hand when I see how much of my stomach is exposed.

But it garners a nod from Kelsie, and Gracie whistles in appreciation.

"Much better. Now, wear these and I think you are set."

She hands me a pair of her boots—with heels, I might add—and I put them on begrudgingly.

I hold my arms out. "Good? Acceptable? Can we get this party started now?" I take the flask from Grace and chug a shot's worth of tequila, coughing a bit after swallowing.

"That's strong," I manage to choke out between coughs.

Gracie laughs. "Oh, my little Padawan. You have so much to learn." She takes the flask from me and does a shot before handing it to Kelsie, who downs the rest and then reaches into her sock drawer to pull out a bottle and refill it.

"I'm going to freeze to death," I state dryly, but agree with their opinions as I stare at myself in the mirror.

"But you'll die looking adorable," Kelsie assures me a wink.

I shake my head as Kelsie grabs my hand. "Come on, Lucy. It's going to be a fun night. You can't stay in your tower all the time. How will the right prince find you?"

"Maybe, I'm not looking for the prince right now? Honestly, I just want to focus on school. There will be plenty of time for boys later. And it's not a tower, it's a library," I state as I stare at her, deadpan.

"Damn, your parents really brainwashed you into believing that, didn't they?" Kelsie says as she grabs my wrist and jerks me toward the door. "Don't worry. You're allowed to have one night of fun per semester, so let's go."

I scowl as I let her drag me out the door, Gracie following behind us and giggling a drunken chuckle.

* * *

"I can't feel my fingers," I mutter as I run my hands up and down my arms for what feels like the thousandth time since we arrived at the game. I'd never admit it out loud, but it isn't all that terrible.

Gracie passes me her boob flask and I take another shot. It's the only thing that seems to keep the chill away. It also makes me feel relaxed for the first time all semester. Maybe my friends are onto something here. I've been so busy studying and trying to keep up on my grades that I haven't been very fun to be around.

"But the nachos...you have to admit these nachos are killer," Kelsie says as she stuffs another one in her mouth.

"I mean, it beats the nasty ones from the cafeteria," I offer, curling my lips up in disgust.

The crowd moves from a constant chant to an all-out roar. I look down to see what all the fuss is about and notice that number twenty-eight has just caught the football mid-air and is running toward the goal post. All the students in our section are on their feet and cheering his name.

Hudson. Hudson. Hudson.

I knew Emmett played football but never even bothered to find out what position he played or even thought about him playing on the field tonight. I might have even missed him out on the grid with all the other players, since my attention has been zeroed in and focused on Hendy, but Gracie nudged me, pointing him out.

And now the buzz of the excitement around me is palpable and I find myself quietly chanting his name along with everyone else. So, this is what I missed out on when I hid beneath the bleachers in high school and calculated stats for the team.

I close my eyes and listen, the sounds vibrating through me like an electrical current. When the cheers become even louder, I open my eyes to find Emmett Hudson in the end zone surrounded by his teammates who boost him up in the air in celebration.

"We won!" Gracie screeches, giving high-fives to Kelsie and everyone else around her, like we had anything to do with it. Then she holds up her hand to me. I give her the mandatory high five before other students around us join in on the action and suddenly we're being swarmed by celebrating fans as we make our way down to the bottom of the section.

"Come on, let's get out of here before we get stuck in the crowd," Kelsie suggests as she passes us the last of the nachos and guides us through the throngs of celebratory students. We scarf them down and continue onward out of the stadium. It's a four-block walk back to Greek Row where we're headed tonight. The crowds thin a bit as we move farther from the stadium toward the tree-lined neighborhood, yet the hum of the joyful masses can still be overheard. At least our brisk walk has warmed up my arms. I glance over at my friends, who seem completely oblivious to the chill in the late fall air.

Gracie grabs my arm and links it with hers and links her other arm with Kelsie. We walk like this a few more blocks until we reach the Delta Kappa house.

Loud music is already emanating from inside, a deep thumping bass rhythm rattling the front windows. A dozen or so people sit on the front porch chatting and laughing, red Solo cups in hand. This is literally the first frat party I've attended this year, the last one being a homecoming party the girls dragged me to last year. I felt so awkward the entire time. Everyone talked about things I knew nothing about—the latest shows they had binged on Netflix, the last football game, who was dating who. None of that was on my radar.

After that, I made up so many excuses as to why I couldn't go to more parties that eventually Kelsie and Grace gave up, leaving me to my studying at the library on Friday or Saturday nights. But when they asked me again this week, I decided I was tired of being alone and wanted to give it another try.

I may not have the same level of confidence as Kelsie and Gracie, but deep down, I still want to fit in. I want to experience all these fun times with my friends.

I take a deep breath and follow them up the stairs and inside. The music is much louder here, which means conversation is going to be difficult, if not impossible. There are a few guys doing a keg stand in the corner of a sparsely furnished room.

Turning my head around, I notice a makeshift bar set up on the counter of the kitchen in the back of the house where people are congregated and filling their cups from a wide assortment of liquor bottles.

"Come on," Kelsie beckons in my ear, leading me by the hand through the kitchen. "Let's grab beers and head out back. They have a fire pit back there and it'll keep you warm. Or...better yet, maybe we find you a hot hookup to do the trick tonight."

When she pulls away she lifts her brows in that very Kelsie manner that says *don't argue with me*. I smile through gritted teeth and shake my head.

We inch our way through the kitchen, the stench of stale beer and pizza remnants wafting around us as we make it to a keg and fill our cups. I take my first sip and nearly gag. It's not very good, but at least it will keep me warm.

I'm in awe at how easily Kelsie mingles with everyone she meets, waving, smiling, and saying hi to nearly every single person we pass as we make our way out back. I'd be jealous if she weren't one of my best friends. She has it all. Tall and slender, long blonde hair and blue eyes, and the kind of curves that make guys always look twice when she passes. And, the cherry on top is she is smart and knows who she is and exudes that confidence.

Me, on the other hand? I'm curvy and on the shorter side. Very, very curvy. It's the Parker woman curse. According to my grandmother, it's been passed down from generation to generation and something I've always tried to hide, even if my best friends tell me to flaunt what I got.

We finally make our way outside and find seats along a stone wall next to the fire pit that's been blazing hot since we got here. A few of Kelsie's friends from one of her classes are here and we start chatting while warming our hands over the fire. I have to admit that two hours later, I'm actually having fun and feeling like I belong for the first time in a long time.

Until there's an uproar inside the house and we all turn to look in time to see several football players making their way outside, surrounded by what can only be described as fangirls and fanboys, the whole group heading toward a beer pong table along the back of the house. My heart nearly jumps out of my chest, my belly churned like it's being tossed at sea, and my palms start to sweat when I see Hendy make his way through the crowd. Wearing a T-shirt and jeans, his hair still damp from his post-game shower, he's graciously accepting congratulatory greetings from everyone along the way. What I wouldn't give to run my fingers through that hair...or down the ab ripples accentuated from under the tight fit of his shirt.

Ugh.

It's bad enough when I see Hendy from afar, but up close and personal? I might just throw up from all my nerves sloshing around in my stomach with the alcohol I've consumed. What if they come over here and I have to interact with them? What if I say something stupid and then Hendy thinks I'm an idiot?

But then my fluttering heart and wild imagination does a nose dive when I look behind Hendy to see none other than Emmett.

Great.

What if Emmett teases me in front of Hendy? Would he even do that? We didn't exactly start off on the best of terms and maybe he would make fun of me for being so uptight.

As I run through all these hypothetical scenarios, the worst and most unexpected happens. Emmett glances my way, quirks a brow, then raises a beer to his lips. I blush from having been caught watching him. He nods in my direction but doesn't smile, doesn't attempt to come over to say hello, just does a slow scan of my body. He then turns away and promptly forgets about me.

I breathe a sigh of relief and finish sipping my beer.

Feeling uncomfortable now in the midst of this loud group and worried I'll make a fool of myself, I glance inside and notice that the family room is now full of people danc-ing. Maybe I'd feel better and less stressed if I'm where I can get lost in the crowd.

"You girls want to go in and dance?" I ask. Really, I'll do anything that will get me a safe distance from potential social suicide.

"Yeah, let's do it!" Kelsie agrees, clapping her hands.

We all stand and walk inside, Gracie bumping against my hip as we pass the group of football players.

Motioning toward Hendy, she leans in to whisper-shout, "You sure you don't want to stay out here? You could talk to him, you know?"

Heat creeps back into my cheeks and I give her the evil eye. "No way. I'd rather just have fun with you guys."

She shrugs but doesn't press further and we make our way into the middle of the dance floor. The combination of the beer I've consumed, and the beat of the music has my eyes closing, my body relaxing as I sway my hips to the techno rhythm while holding my hands in the air.

"Hell yeah, shake that ass, girl," Kelsie teases me, smacking me on my butt. I let out a yelp and open my eyes, my lips turned up into a smile. Before I swing back around, I catch the gaze of Emmett watching me through the window. We lock eyes for a brief second and my breath seems to catch in my throat. But then he quickly turns away to resume his conversation with Hendy. I spin around to face Gracie and Kelsie, feeling like the ground just shifted underneath me.

What was that all about? Was he watching me dance? OMG. Is he going to make fun of me?

I shake off the thoughts, worried that the longer I stay here, the more of a chance I'll be forced to face Emmett. Or worse, Hendy.

"You guys want to get out of here?" I yell over the blaring music.

Gracie gives me a pleading look. "Come on, Luce. Stay a little while longer. We're having so much fun, aren't we?"

I had been until my anxiety crept in. I seldom talk about it, but Gracie knows that I get panic attacks, especially around so many people in situations where I'm uncomfortable.

"Focus on me," Gracie insists as she cups my face in her hands, forcing me to look at her. I do. This is the thing she does to bring me back to the present when I'm freaking out. To get me out of my head and stop fixating on the things that manifest my social anxiety into a big gaping hole of scary.

The next thing I know, Gracie begins singing along to the song and I feel myself slowly relaxing again as she nudges me to sing too.

I can do this. Fuck it! I'm going to stay and have fun. I'm not going to remain some social outcast like I was in high school. I won't let that happen again.

Gracie and I sing loudly to a hip hop party song, throwing our hands in the air and laughing together, and the energy pumps and thrums through my body. It reminds me to let go and just enjoy the moment.

As I turn back around toward Kelsie, who is now dirty dancing with a guy, I notice the football crew making their way back inside. Again, Emmett's flat, expressionless eyes seem to home in on me.

Why? Is he mad I'm here? Maybe he's embarrassed that he knows me. Or he doesn't like the fact that I'm here and is worried I'll mention I'm his tutor.

Shit. I shouldn't have agreed to tutor him or to come to this football party. This was all a big mistake.

But right now, part of that big mistake is slowly making his way across the room toward me. And this time, I'm backed into a corner with nowhere else to go.

Chapter Five

E mmett

I saw Lucy the moment we went outside to grab some beers and get out of the large crowd congregated on the main floor. Truth be told, I first did a double take, having not recognized her. I had glanced over toward the bonfire pit and saw a hot girl looking my way, then realized it was her.

She looks vastly different from the zipped-up, oversized-hoodie-wearing tutor I met earlier in the week. The one who cut me down to size with her glares and dismissive tone.

But based on what I am seeing tonight, she doesn't appear to be as uptight as she was the other day. She actually seems to be having fun.

Did I mention she looks hot as fuck?

She's not wearing the bookworm glasses like she did the

other night that cover her pretty eyes. And her hair isn't back in a severe ponytail and she's not wearing a hoodie.

In fact, she's barely wearing much at all. Her tank top is cropped, displaying the firm, supple skin of her belly that disappears into the waistband of her hip-hugging jean skirt that's paired with some knee-high boots.

Holy shit. I can't take my eyes off this new version of Lucy.

It's like a gravitational pull has me locked in her orbit and I'm being sucked in as our group makes its way through the crowd toward the dance floor.

Hendy saw a chick he'd been talking to after the game and wants to hook up with her tonight, so Killian and I follow him back inside to get more beer. A glance over my shoulder already confirms he's about to score, his body pressed into the girl, who giggles at something he says.

Killer nudges me in the arm. "Yo. I'm gonna hang upstairs with Malik and play some video games. You wanna come?"

I shake my head, eyes still pinned on Lucy dancing with a carefree rhythm in the middle of the floor as I move toward her. Her own eyes narrow in a guarded look when she notices I'm nearing her, but she stands her ground.

I like that. I like a girl with the confidence to hold her own and not make a guy chase her. It gives her a level of maturity I haven't noticed in other girls I've met.

"Nah, man. I'll catch ya later." I bump Killer's fist and he pops a shoulder up, doing a quick scan of the room before leaving me to my mission.

Am I even on a mission?

If so, to do what, exactly?

I should still be pissed at Lucy for her attitude toward me the other night at the library. She made a shit ton of assumptions about me, which I didn't correct, but she drew her own conclusions that I was a dumbass lazy jock.

Fine, if that's the way she wants to see me, then so be it. I suppose I've made a few assumptions about her too.

Maybe tonight we can both correct those first impressions.

I make my way through the crowded room, bumping into people as most excuse themselves the minute they recognize me, allowing me room to maneuver. When I finally stand in front of her, she stops dancing and stares up at me.

"What are you doing here?" I ask pointedly, the tips of my Air Jordans bumping into the toes of her boots. A good foot shorter than me, she has to tip her head back to look me in the eye.

Her lips twist in a cynical smile and her eyes flash a stubborn contempt. She gestures with a hand around us.

"It's a party, isn't it? I'm here to party."

I laugh sardonically. "I've never seen you at a frat party before."

"Maybe you haven't paid close enough attention then." She immediately glances away and begins dancing again, effectively shutting me out.

Just then, someone bumps into Lucy and she's propelled backwards, right into my chest. I know it's not her fault, but it requires me to grab hold of her bare arms to steady her, which produces a zing of electricity that travels through my body and straight to my groin. It pisses me off even more that my dick reacts to her so easily.

"Watch yourself. Are you drunk?" I sound like an accusatory dickhead, which isn't the case. Lucy whips back around and glares at me. Rightfully so.

She presses her palms at my ribcage and pushes away,

her response a fiery grouse. "No, I'm not drunk." She yanks at the hem of her shirt, and I catch a glimpse of a black bra from the shift of her top. I swallow thickly and step back. "And even if I were drunk, Emmett Hudson, it'd be none of your business. As mentioned, It's a party."

I'm about to say something wholly rude and inappropriate like the asshole I'm being when someone slaps me on the shoulder. I'm still looking down at Lucy's face as I see the way her expression transforms. Her eyes grow to the size of saucers and I turn around to see Hendy.

"Hey, EJ, what do we have going on here?" His speech is already a bit slurred. He's probably downed no less than five cups of beer and more than a few shots since we arrived.

I twist around to look at Hendy, who already has a different girl attached to his arm. It never ceases to amaze me how many girls he ends up with on any given night. I mean, that's not my style, but more power to him, I guess. As long as the girls do so willingly and with consent and know what they're getting themselves into with him, it's none of my business.

But something tightens protectively in my stomach with the way Lucy's staring at Hendy. And not only that, but how he drinks her in, like she's next on his list. Her face flushes, her eyelashes flutter, and she licks her lips like he's some piece of candy she's been hoping to sample at a candy store.

"Just talking to Lucy here about..." I don't know what compels me to say it or do what I do, but by the time I realize it, the deal is done. "About our date."

I throw my arm around Lucy's shoulders and tug her into my side. She makes a little squeak of surprise, her body stiffening in my hold.

"Our what?"

"Your what?" Hendy asks at the same time Lucy questions me like I'm from outer space and speaking an alien language.

I smile at both of them like I haven't just gone off my rocker. Which okay, maybe I have, because otherwise why would I even care? I don't even know Lucy or her story.

"Yeah, I just asked Lucy out and she said yes." My fingers squeeze into the muscle of her bicep, hoping like hell she'll just play along with this impromptu charade.

I swear to God, maybe I am losing it. We don't even like each other and I barely know her, yet from the way she looked at Hendy and vice versa, I know she has a thing for him. She's staring at him like he's a bright shining star in a dark room.

And it fucking bothers me for some strange reason. I'm suddenly feeling over-protective of her. She doesn't seem like one of Hendy's typical girls. I also get the sense that if Hendy thinks she's off-limits and with me than he'll treat her differently than other girls. Maybe with a bit more respect.

Not that I care either way. *Do I?*

All of it happened so fast, I didn't have a chance to think it through. So now Hendy is going to think I want Lucy, which I don't. Right?

Fuck if I know.

Hendy tugs the girl clinging to his wrist closer and bends down to kiss the top of her head, all the while not taking his eyes off Lucy.

"Well then, have fun, you two." He smiles devilishly at Lucy, who squirms in my hold. "Don't do anything I wouldn't."

You can count on that, bruh.

Hendy lifts his palm for me to slap and wraps his fist in mine, bringing me in for a bro hug, which also pulls Lucy into the four-way hugfest. I hear a loud intake of breath from Lucy and a giggle from the other girl.

When we extract ourselves, Hendy looks me in the eyes and says, "I'm glad to see you're hooking up with someone. I was worried about you turning into a monk."

He laughs loudly and spins around, leaving me and Lucy standing on the dance floor, both a little dazed and confused.

That doesn't last long.

"What the hell did you just do?" Lucy squeals, yanking free of my hold and crossing her arms over her chest. Lowering her voice, she looks around us before speaking again. "I am not going out on a date with you! I'm your tutor for god sakes."

She turns on her heels and starts to walk off in the opposite direction, looking as angry as a roped calf.

I catch up and reach for her wrist, gently pulling her to a stop. "Lucy, wait. Please, let me explain."

She doesn't look my way, but says in a loud, feisty voice so she can be heard over the booming music and noise of the crowd. "Fine. Explain yourself, then."

I move around to face her, dodging out of the way of two drunk kids staggering by us in the hall as I try to find the right words to convey the reason for my actions just now. I'm not sure I can because I don't understand it at all.

"I...you...ugh." I hit my flattened palm against my forehead, gaining her attention as she stares up at me. "I don't know why I said that. You're under no obligation, it was just that...well, do you like Joel Henderson?"

My question seems to throw her for a loop. Her brows

furrow and her mouth opens, closes, then tightens into a flat line.

When she does finally answer in a hushed whisper, I can't say I'm all that surprised. But I am surprised at how it makes me feel to know I was right.

"Um, how did you know?"

Chapter Six

Lucy

Emmett raises one single dark blond brow, giving me a pointed look. I frown.

What was my tell? How did he figure it out? I'm trying to play it low-key, but internally, I'm freaking out.

Here I thought I played it very cool considering how close I was to the guy I've crushed on for three years. I mean, I didn't trip over myself or stumble with my words or even pass out. I'm pretty proud of how calm and collected I was. And yet this guy, this dumb jock, seemed to have read some tell I'm not even aware of and figured out my secret in a nanosecond.

I can feel the blush rise across my chest and over my throat.

"Lucy," Emmett starts, but then looks around, presumably at the crowd of people. "Let's...can we talk outside?" he asks as he takes my hand in his giant one and starts walking toward the back door.

People stare at us. It feels strange to be watched. I'm not used to the attention. As if sensing my discomfort, Emmett gives my hand a reassuring squeeze.

On our way outside, we weave around people talking and drinking from their red Solo cups, a group playing beer pong, and couples making out in every corner of the house.

I take a large gulp of air as we hit the outdoor patio, a small breeze blowing up my shirt and sending zigzags of goosebumps down my spine as he steers us toward a tree-covered part of the yard.

When we are finally out of earshot, he stops and turns to me.

"Well?" I throw my hands up in the air as if this is a huge inconvenience and disruption to my night. "Here we are. Say what you wanted to say."

Tilting his head, Emmett takes a moment to clear his throat, then gives me a look that says *don't try to deny it.*

"You don't exactly have a poker face. It's pretty obvious by the giant heart eyes you gave him just now that you're into him...like he's the best thing you've ever seen."

I gulp and slap my forehead. "Oh my God! How fucking embarrassing. I'm so stupid!"

Emmett grabs my wrist and pulls it away from my head. "Don't do that. We both know you are definitely not stupid. I mean, you're the one tutoring me," he offers gently, and as his warm dark hazel eyes burrow into mine. I swallow under his intense gaze.

Is he trying to be nice to me? A football player? Why is he making me nervous?

I yank my wrist from his grip, even though I like how small it feels wrapped in his long, thick fingers. I shake my head, not wanting to dissect that thought or go down that rabbit hole right now. I have other things to worry about. Like if Emmett figured it out, does Hendy know?

"Why did you tell him we were going out?" I mutter, folding my arms around my bare belly. I suddenly feel too vulnerable for reasons I also don't want to explore.

Emmett scrubs a palm down his face. "I...listen...if you want to get with Hendy, you need to seem...either very open and willing, if you catch my meaning...or in demand."

Oh my God, just shoot me now.

This is such an embarrassing conversation I can't even. How am I ever going to face Emmett again? I drop my head because it's very obvious that I am neither one of those two things he just mentioned.

I am not one of those ball chasers or football fangirls that is going to advertise herself as Hendy's next catch. I am "an admire from afar" kind of girl.

Emmett continues in my awkward silence. "I guess I just figured if I pretended to have an interest in you and we go out, then he's gonna want what he can't have. Catch my drift?"

I draw my eyes upward and narrow them on him. "And what's in it for you?"

His hand falls to his side and he shrugs.

I stand my ground, keeping my arms crossed around my middle, straightening my shoulders, hoping to seem larger than I am. He presses his lips together as if trying to keep himself from laughing. My eyes narrow farther.

"I don't really want to talk about it, but let's just say having a girlfriend gets the guys off my back and gives me a great excuse as to why I'm not around a lot. I won't feel like such a loser if they all think I'm...I mean that we're...you know?"

I raise an eyebrow.

He clears his throat. "My life is... complicated right now, and having a girlfriend, even if fake, makes it less so, okay?"

How can this guy's life be complicated? All he has to do is pass his classes and play ball. What could possibly be complicated about that?

"And what does this fake dating entail?" I ask.

"Entail?" he repeats.

"Yeah, it means—"

He holds up a hand. "I'm not an idiot, Lucy. I know what 'entail' means. But no one talks like that."

I groan and point a finger at my chest. "I talk like that. It's a word in the effing English dictionary. Why wouldn't I use it?"

Emmett snickers and this time he doesn't stop the grin that spreads across his face. "You're adorable when you try to curse like a sailor."

I roll my eyes. "And you are annoying, Mr. Football Player. So now that we've established that, I think we need to set up some sort of contract and ground rules for this so-called fake relationship." I use air quotes. Goddamn air quotes! I cannot believe I'm even considering this.

"So, you'll do it with me?" he asks, then blushes when he realizes what he said. "I mean, you'll pretend to go out with me?"

"Yes, but there are stipulations and we have to make a pact so that neither one of us gets..."

"*Fucked?*" He chokes out with a laugh. I slap my palm over his chest and hold in my own laughter.

"Oh my God, not that!" I shake my head, trying to sound serious. "I mean...agreements on how often we 'go out'. And that there are rules. There will be no sex or kissing." He holds up his hand.

"We may need to kiss at some point," he says.

"Why?"

He groans and lifts his hands in the air palms up. "Because no one is going to believe we are dating if we don't at least kiss in public a few times. That's like, normal. You know, kissing your boyfriend goodbye. Being excited when you see me. It may require some PDA."

I swallow because my dating experience is so minuscule it wouldn't even be visible under a microscope. PDA, or whatever, is like a foreign language and I'm using the subtitles. Like that scene with Ryan Gosling and Rachel McAdams in *The Notebook*? Is that what he wants to do with me?

Suddenly my face feels flushed and I try to cover it up with a hand at my throat.

"Fine, some kissing if the moment calls for it, but there will be no groping," I say resolutely, gesturing toward my boobs and then using my thumb to point to my butt.

His gaze follows my movement with interest, his eyebrows lifting in amusement. "How about hugs and an arm around your shoulder? And what happens if I accidentally graze one of those off-limit parts?"

"On occasion, hugging may be necessary and will be allowed." I state with a nod, wondering if my arms would even fit around his broad shoulders. I'm not sure how to answer the second part of this question though. "As for accidental touching, one strike and you're out, buddy."

"Alright." He chews on his lower lip with an amused smile. "What else you got for this verbal contract of yours?"

I pause and cock my head to the side as I consider his question. What else should be in a fake dating contract?

Haven't I watched a movie about this very situation? Shit, I can't remember. Where are my friends when I need them? Kelsie and Grace would totally be able to come up with a dozen things on the spot.

And then it dawns on me. Will I be able to tell them? Or will I need to keep it from them, too? Because it's one thing to pretend with people I don't know, but those two will surely see through me.

"How many dates? And are we telling our close friends?" I ask.

"Well," he considers, lifting his fingers and ticking them off one by one. "I'll leave the telling your close friends part up to you. I'm not sure I'll tell anyone. I need a date for the upcoming football banquet. And then there's the annual frat toga party in a few weeks. Oh, and if you really want to get Hendy's attention, you should come with us on the ski trip we take every year during our bye week," he suggests.

"A ski trip?" I parrot, my pulse jumping and skittering wildly. "No. No way. I'm not a skier."

Truth be told, I'm not much of anything that requires coordination.

Emmett runs a hand through his hair and looks around, as if checking to make sure no one overhears him. "Oh, come on. It wouldn't be that bad. I can teach you on the bunny hill. But we don't tell anyone about this trip because if our coach found out we skied during the season, he would bench our motherfucking hides."

I bite my lower lip, uncertain whether I can trust him enough to tell him my concern. "I...uh, yeah, I wouldn't say anything. You can trust me."

He eyes me dubiously, still making up his mind on that one. Then he shrugs as if it's no big deal.

"Cool, thanks. And if you don't want to ski, you can just hang out at the cabin. It's a pretty sweet place."

I start to panic and hyperventilate. This is way outside of my comfort zone. Going out for a burger with Emmett is one thing, but a ski trip? That's a whole other level.

"Geez, this is a lot you're asking of me. I'm gonna need dates. Like what's the schedule for these events? I have midterms and papers and study sessions..."

He puts one of his hands on my shoulder. "Breathe, Lucy. The banquet is next weekend. It's like four hours tops. The toga party is in three weeks, and the ski trip is a week after that. You'll have midterm week free and can study until your little heart's content."

I scroll through the calendar in my head, knowing my social calendar isn't all that full and the tutoring will be light. I really don't have a reason to turn him down.

"Okay," I offer up slowly, nodding in agreement.

Wait? Am I actually agreeing to this insanity? Am I really going to go through with this charade just to get Joel to notice me?

Yes. The answer is yes.

Does Emmett make a valid point about making Hendy jealous?

Yes.

Can I stand to be around Emmett during this experiment?

*Maybe. The eight ball is leaning toward a try again later. But another shake might get it to a solid *yes*.*

The giant oaf of a man is growing on me, a little. This is the most I've ever spoken to a college guy alone without sounding like a complete nerd. I kind of like it. It's fun to be in cahoots with him.

"Okay...is that a yes?" he asks.

I roll my eyes again and extend my hand. "Yes," I repeat as he takes my hand in his giant one and we shake on it.

Only when our hands stop their movement, Emmett doesn't let me go and I don't even care.

Our gazes stay locked for a brief moment and I feel my face heat. I don't know why, but something about Emmett makes me feel...needed. Protected. Valued. It's completely weird and foreign, and I'm not sure how I feel about it.

I slowly pull my hand away, wiping my palm over my hip as he stuffs his into his jean pockets.

"So..." He trails off and glances back toward the house.

"So..."

"We should, uh, get back inside then," he says, his eyes returning to me. His gaze is warm as he stares me up and down. I feel goose bumps emerge on my exposed flesh, but I know it's not from the chill.

"Here," he says, obviously misreading my shuddering body for being cold. He removes the flannel shirt he has on and hands it to me. "You look cold."

I watch his muscles flex under the tight, white T-shirt he has on underneath as I take the shirt and pull it over my shoulders. It's enormous and drapes down past my hips. It feels ridiculous to be wearing it until I breathe in the scent of him.

Holy mother of all yum, it smells so good, just like him. Emmett is definitely making it very hard for me to dislike him. How does one hate the scent of chocolate and peanut butter? It's impossible. My resolve has weakened.

"Thanks," I mutter, clinging to the edge of the shirt.

He wraps an arm around my shoulder and leads us back up to the house. It's a foreign gesture for me. I've never had a guy walk next to me like this.

When we reach the edge of the giant cement patio

where a group is still playing beer pong in the corner of the yard, he pauses, turning me to face him.

"What is it?" I ask, raising a hand to my hair and smoothing it down in case it's all messy.

He clears his throat, a look of concern flashing across his face.

"Lucy, once we go back in there and they see you wearing my shirt...people are going to make assumptions."

Is he worried about what people will think of him hanging around a nobody like me? Probably. He's probably scared it will tarnish his cool football player image and reputation.

"Oh, well, in that case, I can take it off. It's fine." I start to unfurl the shirt from my body, but he stops me with his hands on my shoulders.

"No. I mean...are you okay with everyone assuming that we...were just now...you know?" he says, motioning back toward the trees with the tip of his chin.

My eyes widen as I finally realize what he's suggesting. That when people see us, they will definitely assume we hooked up.

"Ohhh," I whisper quietly, tucking my chin to my chest with a nervous smile. Now that's a sobering thought. A college football player and me hooking up. Will people really believe this charade if we go forward?

Emmett hooks his fingers under my chin and tugs my face upward so our gazes lock again.

"I don't want you to get hurt, Lucy. So you need to tell me if any of this crosses the line."

I look inside the windows of the house, at my friends still dancing and enjoying the party. What will they think? What am I going to tell them? How will I lie to my besties?

"What's our...uh, backstory?" I ask because I'm not good at coming up with lies on the spot.

"How about...we met in a study group that my professor said I'd get extra credit for attending," he suggests, "and we hit it off."

I'm actually stunned by his answer. It's smart, like, actually really brilliant. I frown. Is Emmett smart? Nah. That's impossible, right? Am I underestimating this man? Maybe he's a sociopathic liar and I'll end up buried underneath the tulip bulbs this spring.

Emmett waves a hand in front of my face. "Hello? Earth to Lucy?"

I shake my head, clearing my thoughts. "Yeah, that's good."

"Okay. So, we're doing this?" he asks again, lifting a brow for confirmation.

I nod as the last of my drunken vibes from earlier disappear and reality sets in. He holds out his arm and I wrap mine through it.

"I guess so. Let the fake dating games begin," I announce in a hushed voice, pressing my nose in the crook of his arm and giggling.

This is ludicrous, right?

But so far, kind of fun.

Chapter Seven

E mmett

"Yo, EJ. Is this where you been hiding out all week after practices?"

I peer up from the notes I've been reviewing, my gaze first hopping to Lucy, who sits across the library table from me wearing a pair of red-framed glasses and a black and red CFU hoodie, her signature study wear, then turning to Hendy. He claps me on the back giving me that custom smile of his that Killer claims has all the girls swooning.

Hendy stands there with a posse of his followers—Tate Jenkins, LaShawn Benson, both players on the team, and Killer, who is partially hidden behind the crew wearing an apologetic look on his face. Next to Hendy is one of the football cheerleaders, Macy or Maisy or something like that. She practically hangs on Hendy's arm like she might drown if she lets go. I swear I don't know how he stands all the grabby hands and chicks who clamor for his attention. It would drive me crazy. I mean, that's cool for him but I'd get fucking dizzy with the rotational aspect of his love life.

Even if I had the time for girls, that's never been my MO. Sure I've had my share of frat party hookups but I don't flaunt it like Joel. He struts around with his manwhore status like it's a Super Bowl championship ring.

I'm not throwing shade at him or the girls in any way, I'm just stating facts.

I nod up at the guys while I give a furtive kick under the table against Lucy's foot as a reminder to play our parts. She jolts in her chair and straightens upright, plastering on a smile and removing her glasses.

Then she looks up at Hendy like he's the sun, moon, and stars. Jesus, she really has it bad for him. I inwardly groan and school my expression to avoid looking like a caveman who wants to mark his territory.

I throw a palm in the air as a way of casual introduction. "You guys, this is Lucy."

Hendy shifts his gaze to peruse Lucy with semi-interest. I can tell exactly what's running through his head right now.

First, he checks out her rack, which unlike the party this weekend, is currently covered up by the hoodie, disguising her smoking hot body. I'm curious if she does it on purpose or feels self-conscious in her own skin?

Next, Hendy draws his gaze up and stalls at her lips, full and plump. You know those women on Instagram who try to pucker their lips to make them look supple and kissable? Well, Lucy has such lips which are glossed up with some kind of watermelon-flavored lip gloss, the scent driving me crazy since I sat down thirty minutes ago.

I've had a lot of thoughts about tasting that watermelon flavor right off that mouth of hers.

Yeah, my concentration on my assignment has been shit tonight. If Lucy has noticed, she has surprisingly kept mum about it.

The thing about Joel, despite his natural inclination to look at girls as prizes, is that deep down, he's always had my back from day one and is a good friend and an exceptional quarterback. I have no doubt that someday he will end up drafted into the NFL.

When it's just a few of us guys hanging out together, which we did a lot my freshman year, he drops the overly confident persona and isn't the cocky dick he shows to the rest of the world.

But that doesn't mean I'm very comfortable knowing Lucy is after his attention and that her whole goal in this farce is to get a date with him. The truth is, what I know about Hendy and what I know about Lucy makes me pretty sure that they would be completely incompatible. Something about her makes me think she's not very experienced in the guy department. Lucy's demeanor comes across as more than a little innocent and naive. Maybe even a bit anxious.

I fear Hendy would tear her up and leave her in a messy pile of tears and a shredded heart.

Unfortunately, that's not something I can worry about right now. I don't have room to add it to my laundry list of concerns. So, I do what we agreed to and play my part.

I push back my chair to stand and give each of them hand clasps and fist bumps in greeting. "Can't say I've been hiding, exactly. Just been here studying with my girl. With midterms coming up, I have a lot going on."

This prompts a reply from Tate. "Oh yeah, man. Shit, I

have a ten-page paper due next week on the climate change. Fuck. I might need to find someone to write it for me."

I shake my head disapprovingly and glance over my shoulder to see Lucy's look of horror. Yeah, that's probably not something she wants to hear being a tutor and all.

"I bet if you started on it now, you could get it done," she pipes in, proudly asserting her good sense into the conversation. It doesn't quite have the effect I'm sure she was looking for.

Tate snorts and the guys all laugh. Hendy points a finger toward Lucy, whose face has now turned a bright pink in mortification. Or maybe anger. It's hard to tell with her. She's a spitfire when she wants to be.

"You're funny." Hendy says with a chuckle. "And cute."

I clear my throat, quirking an eyebrow with a tense smile. I flick a glance at Killian, who's quietly observing with a tilt of his head. Yeah, I kind of haven't mentioned anything to him yet about Lucy. The last he heard, I was cursing her name as my *"lame-ass tutor."*

"I agree..." I move around the table behind her chair and place my hands on top of her shoulders, feeling the angry tension rolling from her body. "My girl is not only smart and funny, but hot too."

The responses from my friends are a mix of surprise, confusion, and skepticism.

Tate and LaShawn both grunt out one-syllable words like "Oh" and "Huh." Hendy seems surprised, probably because he believes I just asked Lucy out on a date at the party and knows I haven't had a girlfriend since we've known each other. And Killian just stands there, one gingery eyebrow quirked skyward, giving me a look that says, *"We'll talk about this later, bro."*

Hendy finally nods his head slowly. "That's cool. Well, we gotta bounce. It was nice to meet you, Lucy."

I can't see her face from my position behind her, but I feel her shoulders tense up again. "Oh, we've met before." Her tone borders on serene with a pang of sadness.

Hendy is clearly intrigued by this news, scrutinizing her face as if trying to recall where he knows her from. I know where this is going and it's a train wreck the moment he opens his mouth.

"Did we...hook up?" His voice is disbelieving and it makes me embarrassed for Lucy. I squeeze her shoulders.

She straightens in her chair with a laugh that sounds high-pitched and nervous. "Noooo...we went to the same high school. I'm a year younger than you."

And just as quick, Hendy's interest has evaporated. "Oh. Cool."

I hear Killer laugh-cough behind him and my gaze flicks to him. There's no way I'm going to pull the wool over his eyes about Lucy. And he's about to make me sweat.

"Hey Lucy, I'm Killer." He squeezes between the guys and extends his hand to her. Lucy takes it and I see Killian's eyes light up. "So when did you and my dude here start dating? I haven't seen you around."

His eyes bore into mine and I silently tell him to *"shut the fuck up."* His mouth forms a *"make me, asshole"* grin.

Lucy looks back over her shoulder up at me and smiles sweetly. She's pulling this thing off better than I expected and really getting the hang of pretending.

Who knew that this sweet tutor of mine could lie so easily?

I guess I better watch out for that in the future.

"Emmett and I are in a study group together that I run and just hit it off. Didn't we, babe?"

I nod. "Yep. And then when I saw her at the party last weekend, I asked her out and she said yes."

To seal the deal, I bend down and place a quick peck on her mouth. I barely brush my lips over hers and follow it up with a gentle kiss to her forehead.

The taste of her watermelon lips, combined with the fruity scent of her shampoo, has me dizzy as I straighten back up and smile at the still-confused expressions on my friends' faces.

And now my body is wholly confused, as well.

Because it wants far more of Lucy than it's ever going to get.

Chapter Eight

L ucy

I groan and toss myself on my bed, staring up at the poster of a band I like that's on the ceiling tile above my pillow. I have nothing to wear. The dresses from high school were sized for my high-school boobs. They weren't exactly tiny, but then I went to college and apparently my freshman fifteen went straight to my boobs and my ass. And this year I haven't had an occasion or reason to purchase a new dress, so the only two I own look completely unacceptable

"What's got your undies in a bunch?" Grace asks as she glances up from her desk where she's applying her make-up.

"Literally, my undies...and clothing options. I should have gone shopping. I can't believe I'm even saying that out loud."

Grace laughs. "Uh, why would you need to go shopping? For what?"

"Dresses." I glance down at my boobs. "And new bras."

Her dark, almost onyx eyes, narrow in confusion. "For what?"

"The football team's having a banquet."

I had casually mentioned that I was sort of seeing Emmett to both Grace and Kelsie after the party. Kelsie is over-the-moon excited for me. Grace has questioned it all week long, knowing how much I crushed on Hendy all this time. To say she seems suspicious is an understatement.

"You want to borrow one of mine?" she asks, jumping up from the desk and opening up her wardrobe door. I laugh. It's hilarious that she thinks I could fit into her clothes if I can't even fit into mine. Grace is a delicate little stick figure. She's also four inches shorter than me, and can still shop in the juniors section.

I raise an eyebrow.

With a wave of her hand, she relents. "Fine, maybe Kelsie has something."

"What do I have?" Kelsie asks as she opens the bathroom door and walks out with a towel wrapped around her body and another towel in her hand she's using to dry the ends of her hair.

"A dress?" I ask. "For a thing I'm attending tonight." Just saying this much about the event with Emmett has my stomach roiling with nerves.

"What event?" she inquires suspiciously, like she's a prosecuting attorney on an episode of *Law & Order*, drawing out the words while her eyes drilled holes in my head to get me to talk and admit the truth.

I grab my pillow and smash it over my head, muffling the answer to her question.

"*Th-fooball-banket*," I mutter indiscernibly against the fabric, the words coming out distorted and slurred like I just had my fourth shot of tequila. For the record, I've never drank that much tequila.

The pillow suddenly flies out of my hands and Kelsie's face hovers over mine, her eyes filled with shock, as if she just learned I was a princess from another country.

"You're going to the football banquet?" she asks excitedly. "*Our* football team's banquet?"

I sigh and give her an exaggerated smile. "Yep." I answer, letting the "P" pop.

"O-M-G! What the hell, Luce? Girl! Why is this the first we've heard of it? You need to look *good*. Like yearbook photos will be taken *good*. Like local media could be there. Heck, ESPN could be there," she prattles on as she scurries to her closet and begins yanking out clothing and tossing it on her bed. "We should have started planning for this days ago."

She pauses with a black dress in her hand, humming under her breath as if she just struck gold before she looks back over her shoulder at me with a dreamy expression.

"I was saving this for a special occasion, but shit, if this isn't the right dress for the right occasion then I don't know what is."

She lays the dress on the foot of my bed and nods toward it. "Try it on."

Turning quickly, she leans back into her closet and pulls out a pair of way-too-high heels. They dangle from her index finger by straps that look like torture devices. "With these." She drops the shoes in my lap.

"Seriously?" I mutter, shaking my head. "No flipping way."

"Oh, yes way. Go on...and then I'll do your hair and

make-up. How much time do I have?" Reaching in her bureau drawer for a pair of underwear, she pulls them up before dropping her towel and pulling an oversized T-shirt over her head. Kelsie is not shy about her body...at all. I had to train her to put on her underwear for our sake instead of walking around butt-ass naked.

"Uh, in like an hour," I say with a shrug. I turn and let my legs dangle over the side of my elevated twin bed.

"What? You better get a move on. Hurry up." She motions for me to get changed. I groan and take the dress, underwear, and heels to the bathroom. I begrudgingly shave and use the fancy soap that Grace is always telling me to try. It does smell good. Then I slather myself in lotion and get dressed. Thank God my boobs aren't any larger than they are because this dress doesn't have much give or allowance for a bra. The spaghetti straps lead down to a plunging V neckline. The waist clings to my curves and a large slit in the leg stops mid-thigh. A detailed crystal beaded pattern of flowers runs up one side of the dress. I turn and look in the full-length mirror that adorns the bathroom door, and stare in awe at my backside. You can almost see down to my ass where the fabric gathers in a crescent-shaped arc.

I open the door. "Kels, this dress is..." I trail off as I watch Grace and Kelsie's faces light up.

"Hot damn, Lucy. You look beautiful!" Grace says with wide eyes and a gaping jaw.

"I'd definitely fuck you if I swung that way," Kelsie adds, fanning her face with her hand and letting out a low whistle. "Put on the shoes."

I attempt to but the straps are impossible to work with as I try to stand on one leg. Grace comes over to assist, crouching down to help.

"There," she says when she finishes buckling me in. She sits back on her heels and scrutinizes her handy work. "We need to paint your toenails. Hold on. I have just the shade."

I sigh, nerves and anxiety about even being able to walk much less flash my toes, rushes through my head. "Oh Lordy...nobody is going to look at my feet."

Both of them laugh like it's the funniest thing they've ever heard. Without missing a beat, Kelsie walks over with a large makeup bag and begins laying out her well-stocked and color-coordinated makeup kits. She motions me to her desk chair. "Sit," she commands.

I do as she says while she begins to brush my hair and do crazy things with flatirons and curling irons and Grace paints my toenails. And when Kelsie is satisfied with my hair, she moves onto my face.

"Damn, Lucy. You have the prettiest eyes," she says. Her tongue peeks out between her lips in serious concentration as she layers on mascara. I try to keep my sarcastic comment in check—because it's Kelsie we're talking about— and fear she'll poke me in the eyeball with a mascara wand. It's all fun and games until someone has an eye poked out. Me, that someone is me.

She steps back and taps the tube against her lower lip. "I think a little more eyeliner for a smokier look. I mean, this is an evening event."

"I'm sure it's fine," I insist, waving her off as I start to stand. Grace moves away from my toes and puts the nail polish on the desk as Kelsie tackles me back down like she's a member of the football team. And before I can argue, she's got the eyeliner out and is telling me to close my eyes. I don't know why I allow it, but I do. Maybe I just want to humor her. Ten minutes later, after Grace has dried my toes with a hair dryer, there's a knock at our dorm suite door.

My eyes fly open as a flock of butterflies are set free in my belly. I peer into the mirror, afraid of what I might find, but only see a version of me I've never seen before. Kelsie grins from behind my shoulder and winks. "You look fucking perfect."

"Whoa! You look amazing, Lucy!" Grace assures me.

I stand up and teeter in the four inch heels I forgot I'm strapped into.

Ugh.

How the hell did I manage to get roped into this? I'm not sure I can pull this off. Makeup and hair and dress aside, I'm still me. Awkward. Nerdy. Me. While my glasses and books are parked on my desk, I'm still the same girl just in different clothes. I'm not going to fool anybody.

Tonight is probably going to be a disaster.

I glance over in the mirror one more time while Grace rushes to get the door, letting out a squeal of excitement before she opens it. The girl looking back at me in the mirror looks like a contestant on one of those makeover shows.

I'm pretty sure I hate everything about it.

I'm about to say the hell with this and wipe the shit off my face, when I gingerly turn to see Emmett standing in the doorway of our bedroom, donned in a navy blue suit and crisp white dress shirt and tie.

He clears his throat. "Wow, Lucy. Just...you look gorgeous."

I can feel the heat crawling up my neck to my cheeks. "Uh, thanks. So do you. I mean not gorgeous, but nice. I mean good."

Oh my God, I'm tripping over my words just as much as I'll likely trip over my own feet. I'm so fucking nervous. Thankfully, Kelsie jumps in.

She shoves a small black purse into my hand and leans towards me. "I added something in there...just in case," she whispers, nudging my shoulder conspiratorially. Then she adds with a chirp. "Well, you two kids have fun! We won't wait up."

I want to die from embarrassment. Is that possible? Yeah, it might be.

"You got everything? Should we head out?" Emmett asks as he raises an elbow for me to slip my arm through.

I nod and gladly accept his arm because Lord knows I'm going to need him for physical support if I plan on staying upright in these monstrosities of shoes.

"Bye!" Both my roommates yell in giddy unison as the door shuts. I can hear squeals and giggles erupting behind the closed door and I groan in mortification.

"They are..." He trails off.

"Annoying? Over the top? Going to die after this?" I suggest. But I know I wouldn't have been able to pull this off without their help.

He gives me the sweetest smile and my tummy flips. "Good friends?"

I grin in spite of myself. "That they are."

We walk down the dorm hall in silence. A few people stop and do double takes, amazed at either my transformation or the fact that I'm hanging on for dear life to one of our star football players. I try my best to ignore them and am thankful when the elevator doors open and no one is inside. Emmett presses the lobby button and we stand so close my arm still wrapped in his, that I can feel his body heat. He leans down as we begin to move so that I can feel his breath on my earlobe.

"You do look absolutely stunning," he whispers.

I swallow, his words weaving through me as my legs

clench together upon their impact. Why am I reacting this way to Emmett? It's probably some sort of weird physiological response to his pheromones or something. Biology, nothing more. I steady my breathing once I realize it's become shallow. Yes, pheromones, that's it.

"Thank you," I manage as the doors open and Emmett leads us out to his car, an older model Hyundai. He opens the passenger door and helps me inside before walking to the driver's side. We don't say anything substantial as we drive to the other side of the campus.

"Is the dinner in the arena?" I ask, realizing I didn't even inquire as to where we were going tonight. And now I'm going to have to figure out how to walk from the parking lot into the arena without falling on my ass.

"There's a formal banquet hall on the top floor of the arena building," he explains as he parks the car.

"Oh," I answer, suddenly figuring out just how little I know about my school outside of the science building and library.

I start to open the door but before I can stick my stiletto-clad feet out onto pavement, Emmett is there, holding his hand out to offer me assistance. I accept it and he tucks me into his side once more. There's a chill in the air and I know I should've brought my coat, but I don't have one fancy enough to pair with this outfit.

By the time we reach the entrance to the building, I'm shivering. He looks down at me, mistaking my trembling for nerves, and gives my arm a reassuring squeeze.

"You okay?" he asks sweetly. "Remember, you're smart and beautiful. No one here should intimidate you. You're here with me as my girlfriend...as far as they know...and I have your back. We can do this." His eyes darken as they travel down my body and I feel goosebumps dot my skin in their wake.

"Thanks."

He clears his throat, making me wonder if he's as nervous as I am. I mean, he has to make everyone believe that he'd date someone like me. There will probably be repercussions of some kind. Our coupling will surely catch people off guard.

I push away the thoughts and straighten my spine with a confidence I don't feel in order to give myself an extra measure of height as we prepare to enter a room full of giant football players.

"Let's do this," he repeats with another squeeze of his hand on my arm.

"Okay."

I catch a glimpse of our reflections in the glass as we enter. We look like a perfect couple. We may be opposites, but we do look good together.

A fleeting thought in my head and a heart squeeze that wishes it was true, but I shake it off before it can fully form. I don't even like Emmett. Do I?

Emmett Hudson is just my fake boyfriend, my very real tutee who is helping me to get noticed by the guy I want.

I have to keep reminding myself this is just for show.

Even if it feels nice to be walking in a room full of people with Emmett at my side.

Chapter Nine

E mmett

All eyes are on us the minute we enter the banquet hall and head to our table.

Technically, I think everyone is looking at Lucy and the sexy as hell dress she's wearing tonight. It shows off her legs and her boobs like I've never seen them before. I practically stumbled over my words when I picked her up at her apartment and laid eyes on her for the first time.

I'd only had a few minutes of alone time with her when I could gawk at her stunning transformation. It makes me wonder why she covers herself up most of the time with those big bulky sweatshirts which clearly cover up her assets.

Not that there's anything wrong with the way Lucy normally dresses. It just gets me to thinking whether she's self-conscious about the way she looks.

But not tonight. Tonight she is attracting all of the looks, even as she keeps close to my side while I escort her to the table I've been assigned.

"You doing okay? Need to use the bathroom before we sit down?"

Lucy gives her head a shake. "No, I'm good, thanks. As long as no one makes me shotgun a beer or anything, I'll be okay until after dinner."

I snort-laugh at this because I can't imagine her doing such a thing. I mean, maybe she has because I don't know that much about her, but I just can't envision her willingly downing a beer from a hole in a can.

"I doubt anyone will be doing that here," I offer, scanning the room as we walk through the maze, trying to locate the assigned table. "Especially since our head coach and coaching staff are at that table over there. We have to be on our best behavior."

Lucy swings her head, looking around as if in search of the coaches and stumbles forward as she does. I reach around her waist to gain a better grip and keep her upright, tucking her against my side. Mostly because I like the way she feels against me.

"Oops. Sorry I'm so clumsy. I'm not used to wearing these stilts. Thanks for the save."

I clasp her a little tighter, not wanting to let her out of my hold, but then drop my arm in favor of holding her hand in mine. Hers is warm and soft against my callused palm.

We move toward the front of the room, and I catch Hendy and Killian at table three, the same one I'm at. Killian jumps out of his chair and comes bounding toward us like an eager puppy whose owner just came home.

"Dude! You're late," Killian says with a drunken slur in

his voice. "So, it's your fault that I ate your bread. I'm fucking hungry, bruh."

Killian claps me on the back and we bump fists, making them explode simultaneously.

"Thanks for the heads up." I shake my head with a grimace. Speaking of pre-party, he smells like a brewery.

Luckily, I'm not as hungry as my lug of a friend since I ate a big lunch at my grandma's this afternoon, when I stopped over with her meds I picked up at the pharmacy for her. I'd noticed she was low on my last visit and wanted to make sure she had the refill. Which is why I was running behind to pick up Lucy, too.

She didn't seem to mind. In fact, she'd been very quiet on the way over. I'm not a big talker so I didn't try to fill the silence. With Lucy, it was like we were just in the library studying. A familiar feeling that washed over me like a calm feeling.

Killian steps back from me, takes a long, interested look at Lucy and grins.

"Hey, Lucy-Lou... good to see you again. And might I add, you look very tasty tonight." Killian's voice is loud, that drunken sound that makes me check to see if any of the coaches noticed. Killer could be benched if anyone finds out how wasted he is.

I notice Lucy blushes at the compliment. "Oh, thanks. Hi, Killian."

"You know," Killian adds in a conspiratorial tone, which isn't really that quiet. "This is the first time our boy, EJ, has brought a date to one of these events. He was a date-virgin before you."

I shoot him a death glare and he snickers, sticking his tongue out at me and dodging out of the way when I try to smack him. He makes me sound like a monk or something. Or that I can't get dates.

Obviously, it's because I *choose* not to date. Which is why Lucy's here with me posing as my girlfriend.

At least, that's what I tell myself.

This whole fake relationship thing has messed with my head. It's strange because when I'm alone with her, she acts like she doesn't like being around me. Like I'm one of those kids your mom made you hang out with to be nice when you were in grade school.

But when we're around other people, Lucy seems to play the part of girlfriend so well, I forget she isn't. It feels natural.

Like right now, for instance. With her hand in mine, she leans into me, and she presses her body into my side, clasping her other palm over our joined hands.

"Well, he's not a virgin anymore," she says playfully. Her smile widens and her stance paints a portrait of a sex kitten.

And fuck me, I think it's all getting me hard.

I clear my throat and am thankful Hendy interrupts with his own greeting, Killer darting off in search of food.

"Yo, EJ, come sit your ass down. And bring your girl, too."

I place a hand at the curve of Lucy's back to guide her forward toward the seats. There's a low peek-a-boo swoop in the material of her dress that shows off her creamy white skin, and my fingers accidentally graze over the satiny softness of it.

I swear to God, I literally stop breathing until the connection is lost and I move to pull out her chair.

Hendy looks pleased with himself as he drapes an arm

around the back of Lucy's chair, smiling like he's ready to pounce.

"Hello again, gorgeous. Remind me of your name?"

Something in my chest tightens. I know this is what we want —what I expected and what Lucy hoped for—that Joel will see Lucy's off-limits and that will make him find her irresistible. He just can't stand it when he doesn't get all the attention from all the girls.

Speaking of attention, I notice his date has returned from wherever she had been. She sits down next to Hendy, a look of irritation marring her pretty face.

Lucy seems oblivious to the girl's death glare, and her voice is quiet and sweet when she responds to Hendy.

"Lucy. Lucy Parker."

The girl next to him clears her throat loudly, flashing another icy glare toward Lucy before it turns into a syrupy sweet smile. She extends her hand across Hendy's torso toward Lucy.

"Hi, Lucy. I'm Amie York. I'm one of the cheerleaders for the football team, and an Alpha Gamma Kappa sorority sister." Then she turns her smile on me and I remember that I made out with her at a party my freshman year.

She wiggles her fingers at me in that knowingly intimate way. "Hey, EJ. You're looking handsome out of uniform tonight. It's been a while, hasn't it?"

I wrap my arm around Lucy's shoulders, hoping to look natural in this incredibly awkward situation brewing right now. It has the feel of sharks circling in blood-infused waters. "Hey, Amie. Yeah, it has."

Thankfully, Killer arrives back at the table with a bread basket in hand, completely oblivious to the tension, throwing rolls at each of us. With Killer's drunken aim, one nearly clocks Lucy in the head. I reach out and catch it just in time.

"Look what I found!" he shouts with raucous enthusiasm. "We won't go hungry after all."

He flops down on the chair next to mine, takes a giant bite of a breadstick, and lets loose with an obnoxious moan.

Lucy and I turn to look at each other at the exact same moment.

And burst out laughing.

This evening has the makings of an unusual and interesting banquet.

Chapter Ten

L ucy

I don't want to admit that Emmett's hand on the back of my chair is comforting. I also don't want to admit that I like his giant thigh pressed against mine. I tell myself it's just my natural response to my fake boyfriend and part of my role as his fake girlfriend.

Dinner has been served and a coach is at a podium giving a speech. I haven't eaten much, I'm too nervous. I feel out of my element on every level, surrounded by loud and huge football players and their beautiful dates.

Emmett leans in toward me. "Aren't you hungry?" I feel the heat radiate off his body and I can smell his cologne. Why does he have to smell so freaking good?

I shrug and look back at my plate. I feel a little guilty barely touching my dinner, but there's no way I can muster the bravery to stuff my face in front of Joel. What if he thinks I eat gross? Should I eat anyway? I peer over to see if Amie ate anything off her plate. It looks like she may have taken a few bites of the salad and that's it.

"I'm good, thanks," I lie, adding a smile and a shrug of my shoulder to make it more convincing.

Emmett's hand grips my thigh and my eyes fly up to meet his. He gives a squeeze and places his lips against my earlobe. "You look incredible. Every guy at this table wants you. But only you get to choose. You hold all the power. Don't ever forget that."

I blush at his words. He presses a slow kiss to my cheek before turning back toward the podium. I practically freeze at his unexpected PDA.

Does he include himself in that statement about wanting me? No. Definitely not. Do I want him to include himself in that statement? That question gives me pause. But I quickly dismiss it. I have a goal and that goal is to win over Hendy.

My fingers fidget in my lap. Without looking back at me, Emmett moves his hand from my thigh to my hands. His one hand covers both of mine.

Suddenly all the breath leaves my lungs. His pinky finger is right at the apex of my thighs. My body stills. I like the feel of it there. If he knows, he doesn't let on. But he doesn't move his hand at all.

I sit in silence and confusion, willing his finger to move for the next hour, while wondering why I want that when being with Emmett isn't my goal. But he doesn't move it, and when the speeches are over, Emmett slowly pulls his hand away. I'm no longer fidgeting. I'm no longer anxious. I feel flushed but it has nothing to do with nerves.

"You bored yet?" He mouths the question and then mimes with a pretend yawn, hand over his mouth. He quickly looks around to make sure no one saw him pretend yawning.

I shake my head, pressing lips together to keep myself from giggling. He did that on purpose. He did that to get me out of my head. There's definitely more to Emmett than I previously thought. He sees more than many people do. Like realizing how nervous I am tonight.

Since the speeches are done, the waiters bring dessert. I take a look at it and lick my lips. Chocolate cake that looks to die for.

Emmett brings a forkful to my mouth Ignoring my protest as I press my lips together.

"Come on...try it," he whispers, his eyes locked in on my mouth.

I slowly lean forward so he can slide the delicious goodness between my lips. I moan, my eyelids sliding shut as I savor the taste.

When I open my eyes again, Emmett's are in front of mine. They are dark, pupils dilated, lids heavy.

"Does it taste good?" he asks, his voice low and raspy.

I nod.

He takes a bite of the cake before feeding me another bite. I should just grab the fork in front of me and start eating, but I'm enjoying this intimacy with Emmett, even though it's pretend. I'm not even concerned about what the couples around us are doing or if Hendy even cares. I'll figure all that out later.

"When you finish feeding your baby bird over there, we're going to the diner for after dinner milkshakes," Joel says, almost sounding annoyed.

The couples start to get up, allowing Joel to take the lead as if he leads their every move both on and off the field, like he's the king and they are all his loyal subjects.

"You want to go?" Emmett asks as his eyes search mine. I look over to see Joel stand up and take off his jacket, his arm muscles bulging clearly underneath his dress shirt. Damn. He's so freaking sexy. I thought my crush would go away with time, but it's hard not to be attracted to his pretty-boy face and perfect physique.

I glance back at Emmett who's watching me closely. And then they bypass me and there is a hint of a glare in Joel's direction. I'm not sure what that's about but it looks like jealousy.

I shake off that thought because it's ridiculous and I answer with a definitive nod. "Yeah. Let's go."

I see a flash of something cross Emmett's face. Disappointment? Anger? Annoyance? I don't know him well enough to read him yet but I did him this solid by coming with him tonight, so he needs to repay the favor.

His hand grabs my arm as we rise, and he steers us toward the door. One of the men who had been speaking stops in front of us.

"Emmett. How are you?" the man asks.

Emmett smiles. His smile is genuine, which tells me he must like this person. "Good, Coach." He turns to me, realizing he should introduce us. "This is...my girlfriend, Lucy Parker. Lucy, this is Coach Watkins. He's the defensive coach."

I hold out my hand and the giant man shakes it. "Nice to meet you, Lucy. I'm glad Emmett's brought you. You're a tutor in the science department, yes?"

I feel the heat creeping up my neck. "Uh, yep." And then I correct myself. " I mean, yes, sir."

"Well, I'm sure you'll get Emmett squared away in his class in no time. Keep up the good work, Emmett. I hear you are improving in your science class this semester," he says with a nod before waving at a man two tables away. "Well, nice to meet you, Lucy. I hope you both have a good night. Emmett, I'll see you on the field tomorrow," he adds as he leaves us and walks across the room.

I look over at Emmett. He scans around us before gently taking my arm and moving us toward the door. Is he still embarrassed that someone might find out I'm his tutor? I frown as we walk. He shouldn't be embarrassed. Lots of people have tutors.

I'm about to say something as we exit the ballroom, but we nearly run smack into Joel and his date. Joel has her pinned up against a column and they are kissing. Or playing tonsil hockey.

Probably both.

"Fuck man, get a room," Emmett mutters under his breath with a roll of his eyes.

Joel pulls back and grins. He looks me in the eyes and winks. I swallow, wondering what it would be like to kiss him after having dreamt of it for so long.

"What? Why don't you show us how it's done then?" Joel taunts.

"We don't need to," Emmett growls as he pulls me into his side.

Joel laughs. "Sure. You don't need to, but why wouldn't you? I mean, if you need me to demonstrate how it's done..." Joel trails off as he looks at me, his eyes moving down my body as if he's mentally undressing me. I feel goose bumps form on my skin, but my brain goes blank.

Before I can even think, Emmett spins me around. His big hands cup my face, and he leans down and kisses me. The kiss is hard and fast—hungry and demanding—and leaves me weak in the knees and damp between my legs. His tongue prods at my lips, then sweeps in with probing strokes. Although surprised, I open my mouth to allow him to deepen the kiss as I remind myself that this is for show. It's all just pretend after all.

I'm lost in the moment. Every sense I have is focused on Emmett. I can still taste the chocolate cake on his tongue, so sweet and delicious, and I can feel the heat of his body against me. The smell of his cologne fills my nostrils. When I pull back, all I see is his face. And I can hear his rapid intake of breath as he pulls back.

Joel whoops from behind us. "Now that's what I'm talking about, EJ. Don't stop on my account."

Emmett stares over my head at him. If I didn't know better, I'd swear he was mad at Joel.

"Come on, let's go," he grumbles, pulling away from me and leaving me cold where I was just covered in his warmth. I shiver, and he tugs me to his side, arm wrapped around my shoulder.

Neither of us says a word as we head to his car. Once we get there, he opens the passenger door for me and I slide inside, still quiet. I wait until we're pulling out of the garage to speak.

"Why...did you, uh, kiss me like that?" I ask, not feeling like I have to elaborate anymore. He knows exactly what I'm talking about.

Emmett keeps his eyes on the road as he speaks. "Joel wouldn't have backed down until I did. I love the guy but it's always a competition with him. It's better to show him that we're together for real as soon as we can. That way, he won't suspect anything."

I frown as I remind myself that this is fake, no matter how real it might seem, and Emmett just admitted he only did it out of pressure from his friend, the actual guy I want.

"Oh, I see."

"I'm sorry if I caught you by surprise," he says softly, glancing back over at me. I shrug.

"It's fine, I just wasn't expecting it," I reassure him.

Emmett pulls down a side street and into a parking lot at the local diner. It's a dive place that's open twenty-four-seven, with a greasy food menu that apparently drunk college kids like to eat. The girls and I have been here several times and I do love their milkshakes and fries priced cheap for college kids like us.

"Do you think everyone believes us?" I ask when he stops the car.

He puts it in park and looks over at me. "I don't see why not. They have no reason not to. You're the first girlfriend I've had since freshman year."

"Well, that's good," I say, reminding myself of why we are here in the first place.

He opens the door and gets out of his side of the car, quickly moving to my side to assist me out.

"Here take this. It's cold," he says as he hands me his jacket, placing it over my shoulders.

"Thanks."

"Can't have my girl cold, can I?" he asks, placing his big hand on the small of my back to guide me toward the door of the diner. My feet ache and I wish I could take these heels off as each step feels like torture. How do women wear these things all the time?

I tense up when we enter, bombarded by the sounds of at least a dozen football players and their dates inside. It's loud and at least half the people seem drunk. I grimace. The poor diner staff have to put up with a lot. Small circles from Emmett's fingers on my back calm my nerves, and we locate a table in the corner.

"Let's get us some milkshakes," he says as the waitress

comes over to give us the menus and waters. "You barely picked at your dinner, and it sure wasn't enough for me." Emmett pats his stomach, drawing my attention to the flat tight muscles underneath his shirt. I haven't seen them, but I definitely felt them earlier when I placed my hand on his chest. I can only imagine how perfect they must look.

The question posed to me from the waitress grabs my attention away from my dreamy thoughts.

"What'll ya have?" she asks. My gaze flies to her and I can feel a blush across my cheeks. She's at least sixty, with a no-nonsense scowl, and from the sound of her voice, she smokes a pack a day.

"A chocolate milkshake and a side of fries, please."

"Same here," Emmett says. She nods and walks away, her therapeutic rubber-soled shoes squeaking against the floor.

The bell on the door announces new customers and we both look over to see Joel walking into the diner with his date in tow, one arm slung around her shoulders. He high-fives a few players before taking a seat at a table on the far side of the room. I know I should want to be closer to him, but right now I'm unsure of what to say or do around him. I need to come up with a better plan if I'm ever going to get him to even notice me.

As if reading my mind, Emmett reaches a hand across the table to cover mine and squeeze it. "Don't worry. He's already interested."

"What?" I ask just as the waitress sets down our fries and shakes. "That was fast."

I'm not sure if I'm referring to the food delivery or Hendy's supposed interest in me.

"I caught him watching you at least five times tonight. Trust me...he's interested."

"Oh." I don't know what else to say, so I pick up a fry and dunk it in my milkshake before eating it.

"What are you doing?" Emmett says, making a face and motioning to my milkshake-covered French fry.

I laugh. "Try it."

"Uh, no thanks."

"Chicken," I cajole, making a mock clucking noise.

Emmett glares at me as he picks up a fry and dips it in his milkshake before eating it. I watch his face go from questioning, to shock, to surprised belief.

"Fuck. That's actually good."

"Told you so. Stick with me, kid. I won't steer you wrong."

"Lucy Parker, you are full of surprises," he says with a laugh, gobbling up more of his fries.

I grin. "You have no idea."

Chapter Eleven

Emmett

I wake up on Monday morning sporting a hard-on.

This is not unusual. Most mornings start the very same way.

But what's got me a little freaked out on this particular morning is that my stiffy is due to a dream featuring my hot-as-fuck tutor, Lucy Parker.

She was on top of me naked, her luscious boobs swaying in front of my face before she slid down between my legs to say good morning with her mouth.

Fuck.

There's no way I'm going to make it to team workouts today without first taking care of this little inconvenience. I smirk a bit—technically, there is nothing little about my cock.

I slip my hand down the front of my abs and into my loose-fitting shorts, wrapping my fist around my erection.

Images of Lucy from the other night stir in my head as I stroke through each memory. Visions of her in that black dress, her full, pert tits sculpted against the material. Each time she moved, it gave me glimpses of her cleavage down the low-cut V in the front.

And then that hot as hell kiss we shared. Holy shit. It was just supposed to be for show but her lips were soft and plump, her mouth hot and wet. I nearly popped a boner right there in front of Joel and everyone.

All of those things about Lucy are sexy. But what truly did me in that night was our fake date at the diner when she shared her trick of dipping her fries in the milkshake. Yeah, it tasted great, but that's not what captivated me.

I was entranced as I watched with hooded eyes the way Lucy's eyes lit up when she dipped the fries into her shake and brought the fry to her mouth. Her lips parted, her tongue peeked out, and then she sucked it between her teeth with such zeal that it was all I could think about the rest of the night.

Which literally sucked, because when I dropped her off at her door, I couldn't do anything about it.

I wanted to kiss her again. This time for real.

But I didn't dare.

Lucy has made it clear that the only reason she's pretending to be my girlfriend is to gain Hendy's attention. Because I told her it would work.

And it has. All day yesterday, as the guys sat around the house watching Sunday football, he peppered me with questions about her.

It started to piss me off.

I shake off the thoughts and refocus on my fantasy of Lucy riding me, my hand jerking over my cock now faster as my body tightens and I come all over my stomach with a muffled groan.

Afterwards, I shower and change, then head downstairs for breakfast. When I enter the kitchen, I see Killer at the sink, wolfing down what is probably his third bowl of cereal, and Tate is at the table, frantically finishing up what looks like an assignment that's coming due.

"Morning," I mumble. I open the fridge to get the OJ out and pour myself a full glass, Then I check the cupboard in search of something quick to eat.

Tate's mom is local and once every two weeks drops by an order from Costco of protein bars and drinks, along with homemade food for all of us.

It makes me wish my grandma could do that for me. There is no doubt in my mind that she would if she were able.

Tate glances up at me from his laptop. "Hey," he says before his eyes quickly return to his work.

Killer grins with a mouthful of cereal. "How come your *girlfriend* didn't stay the night this weekend?"

I cut him a look that says *shut the fuck up*. He's the only one who knows most of the story between me and Lucy. I had to tell him the other night because he wouldn't stop talking about it, pressuring me for details. And while I trust him never to say anything, his taunting undertone borders on overstepping.

I shrug, rifling around in the cupboard for my favorite protein bar, the one with yogurt and blueberries. Finding one, I rip the package open with my teeth and take a bite.

"She was busy," I provide vaguely. I continue to chew,

taking large gulps of my orange juice in between bites to wash it down, and hope that shuts down the conversation.

Tate, who I thought was concentrating on his homework, seems invested in this conversation, and chimes in with a follow-up question.

"So you're dating that girl Lucy now? When the hell did that happen?"

Snickering, Killer pipes up like the asshole friend. "Yeah, bro. When did that happen?"

I toss the empty wrapper in the trash can and wave a hand in the air.

"It's new. No biggie. I like her and she's…"

"Hot," Hendy interrupts as he comes breezing into the kitchen, throwing down his bag on a kitchen chair. "She must've glowed up big time because she said she went to my high school but I don't remember ever seeing her then. Must've been one of those Cinderella chicks who never came out of her bedroom until she turned into a sexy princess."

He bumps me in the shoulder as he brushes past me, waggling his eyebrows. I want to poke his eyes out for suggesting that about her.

Would I have noticed her in high school? Maybe. Maybe not.

"Better keep that one tied down. Others might put dibs on her when you get bored or busy."

My irritation rises in an unhealthy and completely irrational way. It's not like this thing between me and Lucy is real or that I'm totally into her or anything, but to hear Hendy talk about how others, meaning him, might "put dibs" makes me want to punch a wall. Or his face.

I'd never put a girl over my friendship with Hendy, I

remind myself. Aside from his cocky attitude and overconfident swagger over women, he's a great QB and a good friend.

Speaking of busy, my schedule this week is brutal. Daily workouts in the mornings, practices in the afternoons, my part-time job at the hardware store, plus taking care of Nana, I'm at the point of burnout. And I have to keep my grades up otherwise I'll be benched. It was nice to hear coach say he was proud of me the other night at the banquet though, like he recognized my hard work. The only other person that's ever said that to me is Nana.

The weight of it all is overwhelming. Yet, through it all, I still want to find a way to see Lucy.

And not just during our scheduled tutoring sessions.

* * *

"Emmett? Are you even listening to me?"

My head pops up, as I lift my chin from my palms to look at Lucy, who waves a hand in front of my face, her eyes narrowing at me from across the table.

I apologize half-heartedly. "Sorry. What did you say?" Honestly, I don't really care too much at the moment about why fungi is important for plant development and productivity.

Lucy drops her chin in her palm with a sigh. "Maybe we should call it a night. You've been zoning out the last fifteen minutes anyway, and I have a paper to finish writing for my psych class."

My hand shoots across the table and grabs her free wrist. She jolts with the touch and shivers run up my arm from the zap of electricity produced by the silky feel of her skin.

"No, please. I'm sorry. I'm just really tired tonight."

She tilts her head to the side, her assessing gaze taking me in.

"Yeah, I can see that. You have bluish bags under your eyes." Without thought, she stretches an arm out and brushes the pad of her finger under my eye with a gentle stroke.

That may be the first time she's touched me on her own accord. All other times it's been me instigating it for pretense reasons.

When I flinch, she yanks back her hand, as if realizing what she's just done.

"Sorry. I didn't mean..." She blushes, blinking rapidly, her face brightening to a pinkish hue.

I quickly reach for her hand, threading my fingers through hers. "It's fine. You just took me by surprise. Along with insulting me."

My voice is light with the quip but she looks alarmed.

"Oh, I didn't mean to insult you. Even if you're tired, you still look hot." Her eyes blow wide and she slaps a hand over her mouth.

I raise an eyebrow and grin. "You think I'm hot?"

Lucy blushes even brighter and looks away. "You know you're hot. Whatever. Geez."

I chuckle lightly but inside I'm preening like a peacock.

She may be interested in Hendy, but at least I know she doesn't find me utterly grotesque and disgusting. That's something.

Propping my forearms on the table, I lift myself up and lean across the table toward her.

"Does that mean you didn't mind when I kissed you the other night?"

Maybe consciously or unconsciously, Lucy swipes a

finger over her bottom lip before sucking it between her teeth.

Holy hell, that is a fucking turn-on.

Her voice is soft and barely a whisper, but I hear it like she's shouting it from the rooftops.

"Yeah, I liked it."

Chapter Twelve

Lucy

He's late.

He hasn't been late since that first night when I gave him hell about it. I look at my phone again. I've been waiting for thirty minutes, and I've left him three text messages. Part of me worries something is wrong. It's the same part of me that used to wait up to get a goodnight text from my brother after I'd hear a call go out on the police scanner I kept in my bedroom.

My brother didn't know I had one. I had found it in a secondhand shop and bought it. It was my obsession for a while in high school. Not only did I learn about all the goings-on in the small town where we lived, I could also make sure my brother got back safely after an emergency call. That fear of not knowing whether your loved one could be hurt...or worse...is enough to drive you crazy.

I take a deep breath as I toss my bag over my shoulder, and find myself walking slowly through the library, as though subconsciously giving him more time to get here. I drag myself across campus to my dorm, stopping multiple times to make sure I didn't miss a text message from him. By the time I unlock my dorm room door, my shoulders sag in defeat. Chucking my bag onto my bed, I walk toward my dresser to pull out pajamas.

"What's eating you?" Grace asks as she looks up from her desk. The suite is dark except for her alcove where her bed and desk are located. The alcoves are what made us put our names in the lottery for this dormitory. Grace's glasses reflect her computer screen, the only other illumination in the space.

I plop down in the bean bag chair across from her desk and lean back to look up at the glow-in-the-dark stars on the ceiling.

"He didn't show up tonight," I mutter, clenching my jaw as tension radiates off me.

"Ohhh?"

I look over to find she's now turned in her chair with her chin propped on the backrest as she stares at me, waiting for me to continue. My fists clench the fabric of my pajamas before I drop them in my lap.

"I waited for a full thirty minutes," I state testily, throwing my hands in the air in frustration. "He promised he would be on time. I mean, what the fuck? Seriously? I thought he cared enough about me to keep his word. I don't have time to waste on someone who isn't willing to be reliable."

"Well, Luce...you learned a valuable lesson. Men are notoriously poor communicators. But maybe something happened to him?" Grace suggests, always the Devil's advocate, a frown forming on her face as she considers her question. "Do you think he's alright?"

"I'm sure he's fine. But he could have at least texted me. He better be unconscious in a hospital somewhere," I mutter, tossing a pillow in frustration over on Grace's bed.

"Damn! That's harsh, girl!" Grace's mouth opens incredulously over my outburst.

"What? I just...expected more from him at this point. I thought he cared enough to let me know. I would have understood." I punch my fist into the bean bag chair. "I thought we were friends."

And then I realize that he's supposed to be my boyfriend so I quickly rephrase my statement.

"I mean, he is my boyfriend after all."

"Yeah, well, you really ought to talk to him before you jump to conclusions. Just hear him out," she insists, flipping her palms up to plead her case.

"Whatever. I don't have time to worry about it now. I need to go finish a paper," I grouse as I get up and cross over to the bathroom. I need to shower and study before it gets too late.

I have conversations with Emmett in my head during my ten-minute shower. I daydream about yelling at him. I daydream about him apologizing.

And then my daydream takes a very different direction.

The image becomes Emmett pushing me up against the cold tile, his hot hands cupping my face before kissing me, his rough hands gliding over my wet skin as he lathers soap down my arms and legs. His calloused fingers spreading my legs apart as he works the sensitive flesh between them. My eyes close as my fingers trace the patterns my imagination gives to dream-Emmett's fingers.

What would his finger feel like inside me? My finger

feels small in comparison to his. It takes me longer to get myself to the edge of my climax, but the thought of Emmett's erection pressing against me while his other hand caresses my breast finally sends me soaring into bliss. I grip the wall as I slowly come down from my high.

"Wow," I whisper as realization dawns on me.

I can't like Emmett. Not like this. This is taking it too far. I need to back the fuck off.

If Emmett doesn't show up, as per our tutoring agreement, then I have the right to end our arrangement and stop tutoring him. That way, he won't continue messing with my head and I can keep working on getting Hendy to notice me on my own. That is my ultimate goal, I remind myself.

I try to envision Hendy drying me off, but my stupid imagination just keeps ambushing me with Emmett's face.

Sighing, I finish getting ready for bed and pull out my laptop, curling up under my blanket as I start pulling citations for my research paper. I need to stop letting Emmett Hudson rule my thoughts.

* * *

The text message arrives at seven the next morning.

I roll to my side and grab my phone from my nightstand as I rub away the sleep from my eyes. When I see his name on the lock screen, part of me wants to toss the phone and roll back over. The other part—the one that had me worked up and dreaming of us naked together—has me wondering what excuse he might have for ditching me last night. My curiosity finally gets the better of me and I open the message.

> Emmett: Sorry about last night. Something came up and my phone died and I had no way of contacting you. I hope you didn't wait too long. It won't happen again.

My fingers hover over the keyboard icons and I debate not replying at all. After a few minutes, I decide to respond. There is no way that I'm going to keep tutoring him. Not after all of this. Hell, I've interacted enough by now with Hendy that, if he's interested, he'll find me. This charade between Emmett and me can be put to rest.

I nod my head over my decision, as though that action will give me the courage to type the inevitable words.

Taking a deep breath, I start typing on the screen. When I finish, I read through it twice before I hit send. My nerves have my finger hovering over the send button. Fuck it. It's time to stand up for myself. I hit send.

> Me: Your absence makes our tutoring agreement null and void. Find another tutor. And I don't like being stood up, even by a FAKE boyfriend. Best of luck with your girlfriend needs. It's been real.

My finger hesitates over the power icon. I don't need drama today. I need to finish my paper. So I shut my phone off and get out of bed. Time to get back my real life. I pull my hair into a messy bun and shove my computer into my backpack. I need to go hide.

I have a few hiding places on campus. However, my main one has been compromised by a certain asshat football player, so that leaves two others.

It's nice out today, so I decide to go to the courtyard outside the engineering building. I'm not sure what brilliant person thought a bunch of engineering students would want to hang out in a garden area in the middle of their quad, but for reasons unbeknownst to me, none of them ever come out here.

Instead, they stick to the patio section right outside their cafeteria on the far side of the atrium. But if you follow the paths amongst the trees, there's a bench hidden amongst some pine trees just off the side of one path, and that is my second favorite hiding place on campus.

It takes ten minutes to walk there. I find myself weaving around groups of students who are already forming small clusters on the quad even at this early hour. Midterms are no joke. My eyes scan the early risers to make sure I don't see Emmett. I make it to my destination without being spotted. Only Grace knows about this place, so I should be safe from distractions.

Opening my laptop, I start writing. I become engrossed in my work and don't even notice the time until I hear footsteps coming toward me. Frowning, I look up from the screen.

My mouth falls open as Emmett emerges from behind a tree. I try to think of something smart to say—hell—anything to say, but nothing comes to mind. My brain is jumbled with questions.

How did he find me? Why is he here? Why does he smell so good? Why can I smell him from ten feet away? Why does he always look so perfect?

"What? No smart remarks?" he asks, his gigantic frame leans against the tree with folded arms across his chest, watching me intently.

I clear my throat to give me another moment to think.

"I...uh. What are you doing here?" I stammer.

"Looking for you."

"Why?" I blurt out and then quickly slap a hand over my mouth.

I watch as he presses his lips together. I can't quite tell if he's fighting a smirk or keeping himself from saying something he'll regret later.

"You sent me quite the scathing text message. I figured we should talk. Grace suggested I look here."

"Oh." I look down at my laptop because I really don't want to have this conversation, even though Grace recommended that I do. As if she's the expert on relationships.

"Oh," he repeats. "May I?" He steps forward, motioning toward the bench next to me. I nod.

He takes a seat and I can immediately feel the heat of his body against my thigh. I swallow, willing myself to stay strong, even though I know from past experience I can't say no to this man. Either he's really good with persuasion or I'm just a sucker for Emmett Hudson.

I peer up at him from beneath my lashes and I frown. He looks...tired, maybe upset? Geez, maybe something bad did happen.

I chew on my bottom lip as I consider what to say, feeling a little bit of guilt and shame creep up. "Why didn't you show up last night?"

He sighs and turns toward me. "I...look, it's complicated. Just know, I had to help someone out. It was completely unexpected and last minute, which is why I forgot my phone charger. It took me much longer than I thought it would and that's why my phone died. I didn't even realize the time until early this morning. I didn't want to text you in the middle of the night because I was worried I'd wake you. I'm so fucking sorry, Lucy. I swear I would never intentionally bail on you."

I contemplate his words, flipping them over in my head as if they are a coin toss. Heads I believe him. Tails I don't.

"You could have borrowed a phone from whoever you were with," I argue, secretly wondering if it was a girl he was with all night. I scratch that from my thoughts because even if he was, it'd be none of my business.

He shakes his head. "They don't have one."

"Oh." I frown again. Who the heck doesn't have a cell phone? Now I'm really suspicious.

Damn it. I have no reason to be jealous of Emmett's love life. I have no claim to it. I am being ridiculous.

"I...I promise I'll explain one day, Lucy. I just can't right now, Okay?"

I find myself nodding, even though I don't want to. I want to ask more. Find out why he won't open up to me. Find out why he stood me up and made me feel all weird about what's going on between us.

But I keep quiet and don't push him any further.

"Will you please give me another chance? Please, Lucy. I'm so fucking sorry," he begs, his hand reaching up and gently cupping my cheek. His thumb brushes along my jaw as his eyes search mine. My breath hitches and my heart races.

The ball's in my court. I just need to decide whether to pass it off or run it into the end zone.

Chapter Thirteen

E mmett

I feel like a shit for not trusting Lucy enough to share with her what's been going on in my life this week. But honestly, I don't want something to happen and her to use the info against me. Not that I think she would but I have seen it with other guys who after a breakup, their ex spills the tea to the world.

This week has been a complete clusterfuck. Everything bad that could happen, did. And we aren't even to Saturday yet. That's when the team plays against another of our biggest rivals, the Central Cougars.

Tensions have been high during every practice, which has meant we've run over our typically scheduled sessions, leaving me rushing home to help Nana with all the things— cook up some meals, and clean her house. Although I'd do it ten times over and choose her every time, it's getting harder and harder to sustain. And I'm trying to keep it all together and not let the chaos inside me spill over.

The worst part of the week was that I received a letter from the Bursar's Office about my financial aid and loan. If I don't keep my C or better grade point average, I can kiss my aid goodbye next semester.

Nothing like the added pressure and the strain of money weighing on my shoulders to keep my anxiety at an all-time high.

But all that was nothing, as I discovered when it all came to a head yesterday. Just when I thought I had room to breathe, I found myself once again gasping for air when I received a call from the Clearview Falls Emergency Room.

They informed me that Nana had collapsed and was found unconscious by her neighbor, Dolores, who had brought over a Bundt cake to share. She'd called 911 and when the paramedics arrived, Nana was awake but her pulse was thin and heart rate tacky, so they took her in.

Thankfully, Dolores knows I'm Nana's emergency contact and called me right after practice yesterday. Which is exactly when I was supposed to be meeting with Lucy. In fact, I'd planned on showing up with dinner to surprise her while we studied.

You know what they say about best laid plans.

Now I'm in a position where Lucy doesn't trust me. Again.

And who would blame her?

She seems to have accepted my apology, but I know I'm walking on shaky ground. The fact that she's allowing me to touch her is a testament to what a great girl she truly is.

I continue stroking my thumb over her cheekbone, entranced by the way Lucy's cheeks pink up under my touch.

"Listen," I say quietly, dropping my hand from her face and placing it in my lap to remind myself this isn't real and I shouldn't be touching her without a reason or permission. "Saturday night after the football game is the toga party. It's the one you agreed to go to with me."

Lucy lets out a little huff. "I remember what I agreed to do, unlike someone else I know."

She twists her neck and gives me a pointed look underneath her long lashes. I raise my palm to cover my chest over my heart.

"Ouch. That one hurts."

She stifles a giggle and dips her chin to her chest. "Sorry. You kind of walked into that one. But yes, I remember. What time do you want me to be ready?"

A few people exit a building near us, their voices and laughter carrying through the courtyard, and I glance over to see one of the linebackers on the team, Marquise Young, walk toward us. He notices me sitting on the bench and stops over.

"Yo, EJ. Wassup, bro?" His voice is a deep rumbling thunder in the quiet area and his bro handshake so strong I have to shake my hand to get the blood flowing again. "You ready to kick the shit out of the Cougs Saturday night?"

I give him a closed-mouth grin. "You know it. We'll be ready."

Marquise looks from me to Lucy and smiles at her. The one that shows off his perfectly white teeth and says, "*How you doing?*"

"And who is this hotness, EJ?" He offers Lucy his hand. She blushes and extends hers as he clasps it in his large beefy paw and brings it to his lips. I roll my eyes.

"This is Lucy..." I pause, choking on the word. "My *girlfriend*. Lucy, this is Marquise. My teammate."

She giggles softly. "I kinda figured."

When Marquise doesn't drop her hand, I reach up and gently pull it from his grip as he laughs. Placing an arm around her shoulders, I demonstrate my affections and play the role of dutiful boyfriend with a kiss to her temple.

And hell.

Now I'm going to smell her fragrant shampoo the remainder of the day. I can say goodbye to any semblance of studying later. My focus is shot.

Which reminds me, I need to get going to make it to my shift on time. My boss at the store has already warned me about being late. I doubt he'd fire me because I'm a good worker and he knows my grandma, but he gets pissed when I don't punch in at my scheduled shift time.

Marquise bumps my fist and we do a quick bro hug.

"I'll check ya later, bro," he says with a nod of his head. Then he gives another glance at Lucy and winks. "Hope to see you again, Lucy."

"Dude, I'm right here. Stop shamelessly flirting with my girl," I chide, giving him a swift shove against his chest. He laughs loudly, twisting to the side with his quick reflexes before walking off.

I roll my eyes and turn back to Lucy, who has a crimson blush over her face and neck.

"Wow, he's huge."

My gaze swings back to Marquise as he strides with confidence through the courtyard.

"He's a linebacker. They're built bigger than the rest of us."

I return my attention back to Lucy who sits quietly next to me. My arm is still conveniently slung over her shoulder. I know I need to let go but I can't seem to find the will to do it.

Lucy's voice is a mere whisper. "I think this is working."

"What is?" I furrow my brows and drop my arm, folding my hands in my lap in front of me.

"The attention. It's crazy how before any of this"—she gestures between us—"I was absolutely invisible to guys. Like, no one gave me a second glance or openly flirted with me like they do now. It's mind-blowing how this has changed the way guys see me."

Something tightens inside my stomach like a bolt being screwed and locked in place. None of what she just said makes me happy to hear, even though it's what I figured would happen.

"Lucy," I say, my finger brushing a strand of her hair and tucking it behind her ear. "It has nothing to do with me. I promise you that. You're beautiful and smart."

She snorts, slapping a palm against her thigh. "*Riiight.* You're delusional."

I swivel in my seat to face her and cup her cheeks in my hands. Her light brown eyes flare wide in bewilderment but then close the minute I claim her mouth, crushing my lips to hers.

Her lips are warm and soft, curving to fit mine so perfectly. As if they were made for me and only me.

My mouth covers hers hungrily and I kiss her with an intensity level that should remove all her doubts and insecurities from her mind. I want her to know with blinding clarity that she is worthy and perfect.

Even if that perfection is meant for someone else.

Chapter Fourteen

L ucy

I fidget as Emmett and I walk the two blocks to the frat party. I feel like an idiot wearing this sheet, knowing I'm practically naked underneath it.

"Are you sure everyone is going to be dressed like this?" I ask for the third time since he picked me up at my dorm room. Although, I will admit, the way his eyes drank me in when he saw me at the threshold had me glad I wore the tiny scrap of lace panties that I'd picked out recently at Kelsie's insistence.

He gives my hand a reassuring squeeze, the warmth traveling up my bare arm. "Yes. Of course."

A car door slams and I glance over to see Hendy getting out of his car. He sports a toga as well, the white cloth clinging to his body and showing off his impressively muscular arms. I watch him look straight past Emmett to me. His eyes rove over my exposed shoulders appreciatively, and I shiver under his gaze.

Memories flood my brain as we stare at each other.

"Out of the way, nerd," Rick Westword mutters as his shoulder bumps me and I go flying into my locker. Rick—or "Westy" as his teammates call him—is best friends with Hendy. Hendy might be arrogant, but Westy is a total asshole. His only interactions with me have been to make snide comments about my appearance or to blatantly make fun of me and my small circle of friends. Hendy is on his other side but he doesn't even bother to look toward me or Westy. He's too consumed by Kailin Harkins, the popular cheerleader that every guy in high school wants to get with.

Grace grabs my arm. "Are you alright?"

I shrug as I rub my shoulder that slammed into my locker. "My pride is bruised but I think my shoulder will live to see another day."

"He and his friends are such asses," she says as she glares in the direction of Westy, Hendy, and their entourage. "I don't know why you like him."

I blush and shrug again. "He's a good guy, deep down," I protest as I remember a time in the third grade when Hendy kicked a kid who pushed me off the monkey bars. I think that's when my crush started. But by high school, we are in completely different classes. I'm taking honors and AP classes and Hendy, a year ahead of me, is in the regular classes. But I know that kid that stood up for me is in there somewhere. I just know it.

"Hey, Lucy," Hendy finally says as he walks around his car. Emmett's fingers tighten around mine. I give him a side eye glance, wondering what that's about. Is this part of his act?

"Hey," I squeak as I feel myself blushing.

"You wear that toga well." He winks appreciatively.

"Where's your latest victim?" Emmett asks with a sarcastic tone.

Hendy seems to take it all in stride and just laughs with a crooked smile. "She's meeting me here. I don't wait for girls to do their hair and make-up and shit."

Emmett hums over this comment, not responding to the arrogance of it, as the three of us keep walking. I can hear people talking as we approach the block where the party is taking place. And then I see them...a sea of college students in white togas. Some even have ridiculous-looking ivy crowns on their heads.

I giggle.

"What's so funny?" Emmett asks, glancing down at me.

"I just...I didn't actually believe that everyone would be wearing these," I say, motioning to my outfit.

"Makes you wonder what's underneath the sheet, doesn't it?" Hendy leans forward and gives me another wink.

I grin and look at Emmett, who's glaring at Hendy. I roll my eyes. This fake boyfriend act is totally working. Hendy has spoken more to me these past few weeks than he has in years. And the way he keeps looking at me...well, I definitely think Emmett and I can have our fake break-up when we are on the ski trip in two weeks.

I really didn't believe this would work, and certainly not so fast. The three of us meander through the crowd, both Hendy and Emmett getting high fives and fist bumps from random drunk people as we make our way around to the back of the house.

The backyard is packed with people dancing, playing drinking games, and standing around something. I step forward and get on my tiptoes to see what the fuss is about.

It's a block of ice the size of a card table with little pathways carved into it.

"What's that?" I yell into Emmett's ear.

He turns toward me to answer, but Hendy grabs my arm.

"Come on, Lucy. Let's do the ice luge," he says loudly as he practically drags me over to the table-sized ice carving. As we get closer, I see people pouring shots from the top and other people placing their mouths at the bottom of the shoots to catch the alcohol.

"Ew! No way! Do you have any idea how many lips have touched that?" I say as I come to a stop.

Hendy leans forward so we are nose-to-nose. "How many?" he asks as a giant grin spreads across his face.

"You are such a boy," I mutter.

He laughs. "Oh, come on. It'll be fun."

He yanks my hand and the crowd clears to let us through. I guess hanging with these football players does have its advantages. Is this what being popular feels like?

"Hendy!" a guy with a gold leaf crown shouts, a bright grin splitting across his face. He's on a footstool behind the ice luge. "What'll it be?"

"I'll take a shot of the top shelf tequila," he says and then looks at me. "Make that two shots. One for me and one for my friend, here."

I pause at his words. His friend? I frown. Is that progress?

Hendy goes to put his lips at the bottom of the chunk of ice and drags me down to copy his position. Our faces are right next to each other.

"Make that three," Emmett says from my other side, his voice gruff and low.

Each of us puts our lips at the bottom of the three

different luges carved into the ice chunk. I glance to my left and Hendy looks over, his gaze locking with mine for a moment. Then I peer to my right and Emmett looks ready to kill someone. What's his deal?

"We got a triple shot!" the guy yells and two other guys step up. Together they each pour a very generous shot down the luge. I don't have time to think about what could be bothering Emmett as I try to swallow the cold liquid that burns as it hits my mouth. I manage to get most of it down my throat.

"One more," the guy calls out and I'm suddenly gulping down a second shot.

The crowd cheers and I slowly stand, but I'm suddenly spun into Emmett's strong arms. He lifts me up and kisses me hard. Whoa.

My mind starts to get a little fuzzy from the shots. I feel Emmett's hands lifting my ass and I instinctively wrap my legs around his waist. I hear hooting and hollering, but suddenly all I can think of is how good Emmett is at kissing. His lips are firm and wet but soft. I shiver at the stubble on his lip and chin that abrades over my sensitive lips. His tongue is both assertive and tender at the same time. The man is a walking oxymoron.

"Stop thinking and just kiss me," Emmett murmurs against my lips.

"But..." I trail off as his hand wraps farther around my ass, moving downward dangerously close to the apex of my thighs. I wrap my arms tighter around his neck. He uses one hand to press my lower back, so that my core is flush with his waist. I can feel his erection against me.

Is he playing? Is that just a physical reaction? It has to be. Right?

"Jesus. Get a room, you two!" Hendy's voice breaks through the fog that surrounds my brain cells.

I pull back slightly. Emmett's eyes are dark as they search mine. I can feel his chest as he tries to get his breathing under control.

"Let's go find someplace more quiet to hang out. It's loud out here," he whispers in my ear.

"But...Hendy," I manage to get out but to no avail. I glance in Hendy's direction. He's my goal. Isn't he? He's been my goal for so many years that I can't fathom giving that up. I want to be Kailin Hawkins from high school. I want to be the popular girl that gets the popular guy.

But does that even matter now because I like Emmett. A lot.

Emmett has been giving me the attention I've craved. Kissing me and making me feel so good that all I want to do is be with him, to feel his lips on mine and have his hands on my body.

But he's not my endgame.

I ignore the confusion that clouds my brain. I look back into Emmett's eyes, eyes that are now hooded with what looks like lust and maybe something else.

"Hendy needs to get jealous. And I know just how to do it," he says, his breath hot against my ear. "Do you trust me?"

Goosebumps dot my skin and I glance over again at Hendy, who is watching us closely. I can't tell if he's jealous or just curious.

"Okay," I murmur. "Yeah I trust you."

"That's my girl," Emmett says as he carries me into the house. I look over his shoulder as he opens the door. Hendy is still watching me, although a blonde is now clinging to his side. He doesn't pay her any attention as our gazes lock again, but this time it doesn't feel the same as it did before.

This time I'm consumed by Emmett.

And then the door shuts behind us and we're inside. It's darker in here but not much quieter with the music blaring. There are people, but not as many as were outside.

"It's not much better in here," I say with a smirk as I pull back to look at Emmett, who is still walking as if he has a specific destination in mind.

"The boys don't like people in the house during parties. Guests use the bathroom connected to the garage. But these are my friends, so we can go in search of somewhere else," he explains.

"Where exactly are we going? And I can walk, you know?"

Emmett squeezes my ass and catches my eye. "Maybe I like carrying you."

"But...we're alone now. We don't have to pretend," I whisper as I glance around. A few small groups of people are in the kitchen talking and sitting on the sofas in the living room. A couple makes out on a lounge chair in the corner, the guy's hand disappearing up the girl's toga, and a few couples dance slowly in the middle of the room.

"Consider this practice for when you're with him," Emmett says.

"Practice?" I ask.

"He's used to...experienced girls, shall we say," Emmett explains.

"Oh. Are you?"

He stops walking and looks down at me. "Experience doesn't matter to me. But I have had my share of it." He presses his forehead against mine. "Consider me your tutor for the night. But only if you want to."

I shiver under his intense gaze. Is this a good idea? Nope. Definitely not. Little warning sirens blare in my brain, but the tequila shots deafen them. Maybe he's right. And who better to practice with than Emmett? After all, I've come to trust him.

I swallow and decide to just go with it. To stop over-thinking everything I do with a guy and let go. "Okay. I'm the student tonight and you're the teacher."

Emmett's grip tightens on me. "Fuck, Lucy. That's a hot scenario."

I giggle. "Okay, Professor Hudson. Teach me."

Chapter Fifteen

Emmett

Holy shit. Did she just agree to do what I've been thinking about doing with her all night?

After the shit Hendy pulled outside, I was immediately in the mood to either fuck or fight, and I figured neither was going to happen tonight.

The best thing for me to do was get the hell out of there and bring Lucy with me. I honestly don't understand what she sees in Hendy and, to be honest, I'm getting sick of the way he is constantly flirting and encroaching into my territory. Not that I believe women are property or that being in a relationship means you own one another, but if this thing with Lucy was real, where's the bro code, dude? Find your own damn woman.

It used to be amusing and like a game when we watched how Hendy was with girls.

But now that I've been with Lucy, I know she is not the type of girl for him.

And maybe she isn't the right one for me either, but there's a lot about her that I like. Not only is she smart, although sometimes quirky and anxious, but she's really beautiful and fun to be with.

"Do you want anything more to drink?" I ask, setting her down on her feet but keeping a hand at the small of her back so she doesn't wobble. I think those shots probably went straight to her head because she's looking at me with big, glassy eyes.

Lucy giggles. "I probably shouldn't. I already feel the effects of the last few."

I laugh. "Yeah, I figured as much." I hesitate before saying what's on my mind, not wanting to push the boundaries too far and unable to read where she stands with everything.

Does she like me? Or is this still just a game to her?

And then there's those RULES. When she first agreed to this, she set two very clear rules, one of which I've already sort of broken with the kissing. So tonight could border on breaking rule number two.

I clasp her small hand in mine and turn the corner toward the stairwell, hesitating at the bottom of the steps before raking my gaze over her with a question in my eyes.

"Do you want to go upstairs with me?"

She bites down on her lower lip in thought and I grow hard.

Please say yes.

"Um, yeah sure. That definitely sounds more quiet."

I nod in agreement. "Okay, then let's do it."

I wonder if she catches the meaning in that phrase. Not

that I expect anything to happen, but just to see where she wants it to go, if anywhere.

We take the stairs and when we reach the top I go in search of an open room. A few of the doors are locked and shut tight until we find one at the far end of the hallway. I knock once and nobody answers so I try the door handle and it's open.

Suddenly my stomach is in knots, my nerves swimming around with the shots we just took outside.

As I enter the room, I stop and turn to face her.

"Lucy," I say quietly. "We don't have to do anything. At all. But I will state for the record that I like you. I can't fake this when I'm around you."

I raise her hand in mine and place it over my chest above my heart. Lucy's eyes grow wide when she feels how fast my heart races.

The next thing she does surprises the hell out of me. She takes my hand and places it over her own heart. It's the mirror reaction to mine.

"Emmett," she says softly. "Teach me."

Holy fuck.

Those two words, whether she knows it or not, open the floodgates for my libido, and there is no stopping it now. Well, only if she puts a stop to it, that is.

I waste no time in getting down to business. If we only have tonight, then I want to make it count and get an A+ for effort.

"Are you sure?"

"Yes," she says almost breathlessly.

I raise my hands to frame her face cupping gently as I brush my lips over hers. She tastes like lime and tequila and something sinfully all her.

My tongue sweeps across her lips in a hungry pattern,

nipping and tasting, until I take her lower lip between my teeth and suck hard.

A small gasp releases from her throat and I can feel her nipples pucker against my chest from underneath the sheet that clings to her body.

And holy hell, do I want to get that sheet off.

I move a hand along her spine, dragging my fingertips up and down as they travel over her smooth bare skin. The way she trembles in my arms and underneath my touch has my cock straining wildly in search of friction. I duck my head and place my lips along her jawline, kissing and sucking my way down the slender slope of her neck. Her scent infiltrates every part of my senses. It's like lemon and honey mixed with the sweetness of marmalade. I want to devour every inch of her.

Being with her in this moment makes me forget every-thing else outside of this room. All the stress with my grandma. The nervous tension I have when I play football. The uncertainty of my future financial aid and what I want to do after graduation next year.

She is either the best distraction or the greatest tutor in the world because she's teaching me how to let go of those worries.

"God," I murmur against her neck. "You taste so fucking good."

I strum my hand over her ass, cinching the material of the sheet in my fingers as I drag it up her leg, my knuckles to brush against the back of her thigh. My mind goes completely blank as I graze along her inner leg, climbing higher until I reach the juncture at her center. I feel her heat and warmth penetrating the silky material as I glide along the seam of her panties. My groan is loud and rever-berates against the walls.

"Are you ready for your first lesson?" I ask in a harsh whisper.

Lucy's breath hitches and I feel her legs tremble under my hand.

"Yes."

That one word has my knees nearly giving out.

I don't hesitate any longer. "Spread your legs."

She draws in a deep breath and whimpers, dropping her forehead against my chest. Then, without question or resistance, she opens her legs at my command. I take the opportunity to draw a line from the front of her panties to the back with my index finger, dragging it through the seam of her pussy. Lucy's hands grip the top of my shoulders, her fingernails digging into my muscles.

"Do you like that? Do you want more?"

"Mmm-hmm," she replies, arching her back and pressing farther into my hand.

I chuckle at her eagerness. And if I were a more patient guy, I might tease her even more. But as it is, I'm already close to reaching my limit and I'm not sure how long this lesson can go on before I lose myself.

Using my fingertip, I wiggle underneath the edge of her panties, drawing it across her flesh, her wetness coating my finger. Lucy lets out a small tremoring moan that goes straight to my cock. My very hard and leaking cock.

Seeing that we're standing in the middle of the room still, I glance over my shoulder to determine the distance from the bed. I boost Lucy under her butt with my free hand and carry her over to the edge of the bed, where I drop her onto the mattress. She lands with a soft thump and a wispy gasp.

I look down at her and marvel at how gorgeous she is. Her golden hair fans out over the pillow and her full kiss-drenched lips are parted in an open invitation. The way she looks at me makes me feel invincible.

"You're a good student so far," I comment, raising a seductive eyebrow. "Ready for your next lesson?"

She nods and licks her lips. I give her a wag of my finger and kneel down on one knee, dipping into the mattress between her parted legs.

"I need to hear you say it."

"I'm ready for whatever lesson you have to teach me."

I swallow thickly, my eyes drinking in every inch of her body laid out before me. The only downside is that she is still dressed in a sheet.

"Then your second lesson is to get naked."

Her eyes go wide before a blush creeps up her neck and over her rosy cheeks. Her arms come up and cross over her chest as she turns her head to the side, avoiding my eye contact.

"Do you need some time to work on your assignment?" I ask, a smirk rising at the corners of my mouth.

Using my thumb and index finger, I pinch her chin and turn her face to look back at me, waiting for her to comply.

"You want me to take it all off?"

I reach out and pluck her arms out to her sides before I place my thumb against her bottom lip, pressing gently. Drawing her mouth open, I bend down and crush my mouth to hers in a deep, igniting kiss. When I pull back, we are both breathless, and Lucy's chest rises and falls as my cock nestles between her legs. Then I whisper in her ear.

"All. Off."

I push back up onto my knees to give her room and time to decide if this is still what she wants to do. I want to give her every chance to come to her own conclusion on where this is heading so she doesn't feel like I pressured her into doing anything she doesn't want.

Slowly and intentionally, she raises her hands to the knot that's tied just at the top of her right breast. Wiggling the tie loose, it comes undone and like a butterfly extending its wings, she opens her arms to expose her bare breasts.

There is nothing more beautiful in this world than a naked Lucy waiting for me to make the next move.

And just like football or a game of chess, the next move I make will hopefully be a game-winning one.

Chapter Sixteen

Lucy

I feel the heat creeping up my chest and neck as Emmett gazes down at me. I bite my lip as I slowly peel back the sheet, exposing my entire body. The only piece of fabric left is my panties, but for all intents and purposes, I'm naked and exposed in a way I haven't been in a long time.

The way Emmett stares at me with his hooded eyes is so intense I have to look away.

His finger presses under my chin, tilting my head up so I'm forced to return my gaze to his eyes.

"You're beautiful, Lucy. You're the most beautiful girl I've ever seen," he reassures me.

"I'm sure you say that to all the girls you're with."

I don't want to believe him because denying his honesty is a hell of a lot easier than accepting that Emmett just spoke the truth.

He leans forward and runs his nose along the side of my neck until his hot breath is caressing my earlobe. "Never before now," he whispers.

I shiver under his feathery touches as his fingers glide along the side of my breast and down along my hip. He eases his leg between mine and pauses as his lips graze my chin.

"I meant what I said. You say the word and we stop all of this, understand?" he repeats. "I know this goes against the rules you set."

I nod, not trusting myself to speak, feeling foolish now for making those damn rules. Because tonight I want to be a rule breaker with Emmett.

"Say it out loud, Lucy," he demands.

"I understand."

"Good girl," he praises, his voice low and gravelly. And fuck, why is that hot? Do I have some weird-ass praise kink? No.

Yes?

Maybe.

"Lesson number one. Stop overthinking. Turn that big, beautiful brain off and just feel what I'm doing to you," he commands, trailing kisses down my neck and slowly pushing me back until I'm leaning on my elbows.

Emmett bends to cover my left nipple with his mouth and I let out a shaky breath. As if this turns him on more, he sucks hard enough to make me whimper. He wedges another knee between my legs, seating himself between my thighs. His hands push my inner thighs apart. When his lips travel down to my belly, my eyes grow wide as I feel the hard length of him against my thigh.

"I..." I trail off because I know for sure that my cheeks are now bright red.

He pauses with his head between my legs, his lips pressing to the wet spot on my panties. I nearly fly off the bed but he keeps me down with a hand across my belly. His nostrils flare and I swallow hard.

"Maybe we should use a traffic light safeword system," he suggests. I can feel his hot breath against my clit even through the fabric and I groan. It feels so damn good.

"Green light," I whisper, the words coming out in a *whoosh* between my lips.

"You're sure?" he asks, his thumbs hooking into the sides of my panties, skimming, and teasing the sensitive skin.

"I've never...I mean no guy has ever..." I trail off and shake my head. "I did...it, but not this." I close my eyes in total mortification. It's embarrassing to admit my shortcomings in this particular scenario.

Emmett climbs back up and kneels between my legs once again.

"Open your eyes, Lucy," he says quietly. When I do, he's right there, his hazel eyes looking at me with concern. "Are we still good?"

I nod.

"Let me show you how good it can be," he pleads, searching my eyes for agreement. In this moment, I trust him. I trust him more than I've ever trusted anyone.

"Okay," I reply, biting down on my lip to keep from smiling too big.

Emmett presses his lips to mine in a slow gentle kiss as he reaches down and pulls my panties down my legs. When he has them off, he trails kisses down my abdomen once again. This time, I don't look away. I watch in wonder as he stares greedily at my sex. I should feel embarrassed by the intensity with which he looks at me. But I don't. Instead, it gets me even wetter.

He runs a single finger through my folds, separating my flesh. I let out a shaky breath as he slowly eases it inside me. And then, with eyes on mine, he runs his tongue over my clit.

Holy fucking shit!

I nearly arch off the bed at the zap of pleasure it sparks.

He chuckles and I realize I said that out loud. But he doesn't seem disturbed by that. Instead, he doubles his efforts, sucking and licking until I'm shaking with need. It's like he's trying to figure out the key to unlock something. He tries different movements with his finger and tongue, bringing me so close to the brink and then pulling back slightly before starting again.

I'm panting and it takes everything to keep my eyes open. Locking eyes with him while he turns me into a puddle of need is the most intense thing I've ever experienced.

His finger curls and I feel my hips buck involuntarily in response. He smirks against my wetness, and I want to roll my eyes but I'm too focused on the feel of his rough digit inside me.

"Don't stop, please," I beg. Did I just say that? I barely recognize the sound of my hoarse voice.

His lips cover my clit and he sucks hard, swiping his tongue quickly back and forth as his finger continues to stroke that spot deep inside me. I feel my entire body tense like a rubber band being pulled and flexed. And then I go completely rigid as the most intense orgasm of my life rips through me, splintering me wide open.

At some point, I lose the fight to keep my eyes open. My head falls back onto the bed and I press my lips together to keep from screaming. I'm trembling from head to toe from the way Emmett brought me to a high I never knew was possible.

It takes a few seconds for me to catch my breath, and when I do, I open my eyes to find Emmett kissing my hip. His lips are wet from me, and he runs his tongue over them as if he wants to taste more.

Whoa, that's hot. Why hadn't I ever known that sex could be this hot?

He slowly removes his finger from my wet center as my body clenches once more. He lets out a low growl.

"I think we should skip a few chapters to a much bigger lesson tonight," he says as he places kisses along my belly. He slowly makes his way back up my body until I feel his heavy and hard erection pressing through the fabric of his toga against my sensitive flesh.

We both groan at the contact.

"I don't have a condom," I manage to squeak out, my voice sounding distant and panicky.

He looks around and opens a side drawer, grinning as he retrieves an entire box of them and plucks one from the pack.

"Well, that's very convenient," I giggle as my eyes widen at the size of the condoms. "How did you know they'd be in there?"

He laughs. "I know which guy has this room. I'm thinking his ego is bigger than his..." He trails off with a smirk, flapping the package in the air. I'm left wondering if Emmett shares that problem because it certainly doesn't feel like he does.

Now I am nervous. I've only had full-on sex twice, both times with the same guy. I don't know what to expect from this huge football player.

"Yellow," I suddenly sputter out softly, not completely sure he heard me. But he pauses and looks down with a serious expression.

"Okay. We don't have to do that lesson tonight."

"I mean, I'm not opposed. I just...I haven't done this much, so..." I stammer, searching for the right words, which really are *I'm afraid you will put some sort of giant dick inside me that could maim me for life.*

"Let's practice some more and then we can see how you feel," he suggests with a wink, tossing the condom behind him with a shrug.

I nod and he leans forward, grasping my lower lip with his teeth and pulling it free. He sucks on it for a second and then slowly pushes his tongue inside my mouth where the taste of myself still lingers on his tongue.

Did he enjoy going down on me? Does he like that kind of thing?

I feel his finger tracing my folds before it makes its way inside again, only this time, he adds a second finger.

I immediately tense but then relax as he caresses me with such exquisite tenderness. His movements are slow and gentle as his lips and tongue explore my mouth. I sigh into him as he curls his two fingers and finds that same spot again.

"I think my student might be getting an 'A' for multiple orgasms."

"Show-off," I teasingly reply but he's closer to the truth than I care to admit. Emmett knows what the hell he's doing.

He grins against my lips as he scissors inside me and then uses a 'come hither' motion to curve his fingers, which has my hips bucking again, seeking that friction.

"There we go. Let go, Lucy," he murmurs as he

continues playing me like an instrument. The sound of my wetness is almost embarrassing, but I'm too far gone to care. I close my eyes, my hands in search of something to hold onto. When I latch onto a pillow, I give into my other senses and let go. Within seconds, I'm soaring again.

This time a cry escapes me, but Emmett is there with his mouth to dampen the sounds. When my trembling subsides, Emmett places a light kiss on my nose. "Ready for the next lesson?"

I nod, pressing my forehead to his. "Just...be gentle. My high school boyfriend was not as...big as you."

Emmett laughs. "Damn, you're good for my ego."

I whimper as he presses his erection where his fingers just were. Where I'm hot, wet, and sensitive. He stops laughing and gives me a serious look. "I would never do anything to hurt you, Lucy."

"Don't make promises you can't keep," I whisper.

He looks into my eyes. "I wouldn't dare."

This isn't real. It doesn't matter, I remind myself.

He finds the discarded condom wrapper and brings it to his mouth to tear open just as someone knocks on the door.

"Fuck," he grunts, rearing back and quickly covering me up with my toga sheet that had been discarded on the floor. "Go away!" he yells. "We're busy."

"It's my fucking room, dickhead," the voice yells back.

"Shit," he mutters. "I'm sorry, Lucy, but I think we're getting evicted."

I groan as I re-tie my toga. "Great. Now, I'm going to have a lady boner."

He chuckles. "A lady boner?" I notice his hand lands at his crotch and he adjusts his own boner under his toga.

"Me, too."

Guess I'm not the only one with an issue.

He takes my face in his hands. "Sorry our lessons got interrupted."

I shrug, now suddenly a little shy. "It was a very informative lesson, Professor Hudson."

He smiles at me and places a quick kiss on my lips. "Anytime."

"For fuck sakes! Get the hell out!" the voice yells from the other side of the door.

We both look at it and burst into laughter as Emmett throws open the door and grabs my hand.

"Sorry," I manage to yell with a laugh, passing the guy and who I assume is his girlfriend standing in the hallway.

"My bad, man," Emmett calls out to him.

"Fuck off, Emmett. Next time, just ask," he yells back at us.

Emmett grins and waves behind him as we continue running down the hall and the stairs. As we get to the bottom of the landing, he pushes me against the wall, pinning me with his overly heated body. I can still feel his semi hard-on behind his toga and I want to push forward and rub against him.

I look up at him, and his eyes flash with...lust? care? I can't be certain.

"I meant what I said up there, Lucy. You would tell me if things go too far for you, right?"

I nod. "Of course."

But it's a lie. I'm pretty sure we just crossed some invisible line and broke all the rules, and I'm not sure we can go back.

Do I even want to?

Chapter Seventeen

Emmett

"Wait a minute," Killer says, glancing over his shoulder at me. "So you're telling me you got this close to boning down with Lucy and you got cockblocked by Allen? Dude, that's harsh."

Killian has always been a loud talker but he's extra exuberant this morning, his voice echoing off the high-lofted barn ceiling. I'm not surprised that his voice carries but I feel a rush of embarrassment having a conversation like this in a public arena. I don't normally bring up sex, but I need his advice on Lucy and our situation.

I do a quick check to make sure no one overhears, but the only other living souls are the horses a few stalls down from this cow stable. I shake my head at his question, then lift a foot and place it on the rung of the metal fence as I stare into the pen where Killian is doing his required work this morning.

It's a weird juxtaposition to be talking about sex when he's taking care of three baby calves that are all mooing for his attention.

Because he's on duty to take care of the new arrivals just born this past month at the agricultural center, I knew I'd find him here. I made it a point to bring him coffee so we could chat. It's the only time since Saturday night when everything went down with Lucy—no pun intended—that I've been able to speak with him with our schedules conflicting, so I figured I might as well track him down here to spend some time with him this morning before the rest of the week got under way.

We were just catching up on Saturday night's events when he asked me how things were going with Lucy, so I told him about being interrupted by Allen Tracy at the frat house.

"Yeah, it sucks, but what can you do? It was his room and we were there without his permission. I just felt bad for Lucy. She was so embarrassed."

Killian lets out a gruff snort of disapproval. "Yeah, but still, there's the bro code. I would've at least let you finish." He turns around with a proud grin and a wink, as if he's *ever* done that for me in the past. Usually he just barges right in without thinking or knocking. Even with the tie-on-the-doorknob warning. He just forgets.

"Oh, you mean like what I have to do for you every time you have a girl over?"

He hoots in laughter, startling one of the calves when he smacks his dirty jean-clad knee.

"You're funny, bro." He takes a sip of the now lukewarm coffee and places it on a bench before turning to nod at the far end of the barn. "Hey, can you do me a favor and go grab that feed bag and bring it over for me?"

I turn to look where he's just pointed and nod, lifting the large bag of some kind of stinky-ass feed. No wonder Killian is such a beefy guy if he's hefting these things around every day. The bag has to weigh at least fifty pounds.

I carry it back to where he's standing and set it down beside me. "Now what?"

He rises from his crouching position and turns to lean over the fence, picking up the bag and swinging it over to the other side where I watch him dump half of it into a feed trough.

In a sweet motherly tone, he coos to the hungry cows. "There you go, my little babies. Eat it all gone so you can grow up to be someone's dinner, and I'll see you later."

He pats each one on its rump and even ruffles one behind its ears before opening the gate to step through, then spinning around to latch it tight.

I regard him with disbelief. "I have honestly never heard you use that tone of voice before. It's like you have a soft side or something."

Killian laughs jovially and pats his thick stomach with his hand. "I'm like one of those candies that's hard on the outside and gooey on the inside."

I snort. "Oh, Jesus. Better not let any of the girls know that or you're in trouble, my man." I clap a hand on his shoulder.

"Speaking of girls and trouble, what's going on with Lucy? I thought you said it was all for show. Obviously, that was a load of shit you were flinging since now you guys are doing the nasty? Seems real to me if you are getting down to business."

Killian removes his dirty gloves and washes his hands in a basin against the far wall as I try to decide how to answer.

I could just play it off and pretend I don't have feelings for her, saying it's just sex, but I actually really like Lucy. I enjoy spending time with her. She's smart, funny, and extremely snarky, which I find cute. It's easy to listen to her talk, especially about the things she's passionate about, like the future and what she wants to do after graduation. It makes me want to open up and tell her what I'd really like to do with my life. That I want to go to law school and become a sports agent. But I know that I have no way in hell of making that happen. Not with everything that's going on with Nana, her health and medical needs, and my finances.

The only bright spot recently is that I was finally able to get a day nurse to come in and care for Nana. A huge relief and burden has been lifted from the pressures piling on me like ten defensive tackles.

Even so, I've always been reluctant to share my hopes and dreams with anyone but somehow, I know that if I mentioned it to Lucy, she'd encourage me...because that's how she is.

She'd help me find a way to do it. Lucy is good at seeing the positive in everything and everyone. Except herself.

Which angers me over and over again because I can't understand why she puts so much stock in trying to get a guy like Hendy to like her. She has these hopes of him returning her feelings, but he's not that kind of guy and probably never will be.

And that's why I'm not sure she'd ever want to date me for real. It's like this unanswered question that hangs over my head every time we're together. Saturday night's escapades aside, if I laid it out on the line for her and told her how I felt, would she return the sentiment or laugh in my face?

So I debate on how to answer Killer's question.

"Nah, man, it's not serious. I'm not sure if she's really into me."

Killer gives me a look that says he doesn't believe me. "That's not how I see it, dude. She had all eyes for you the other night, like you hung the moon and stars or something."

I snort-laugh, and the horses pop their heads up over their stalls to answer me with snuffles and neighs.

He bumps me on the shoulder with his as we walk out side by side into the agricultural center yard and toward the parking lot.

"Women," he laments, as if he has so much knowledge and experience in relationships. "I guess you just see how it goes and take it one day at a time. Plus, there's the ski trip coming up and at least you get to have your own bedroom for that. I promise, I won't interrupt your private sessions."

I use my palm and shove him against his shoulder hard enough that he bends sideways with a laugh.

"Gee, what a good friend you are."

"I know, right? Whatever would you do without me?"

"Probably get better advice."

Killer laughs again as he climbs into his truck. "I'll see you at practice later. And thanks for the cup of Joe."

"No problem. Catch you later, bro."

I just got home and showered after another grueling practice and am now sitting on my bed and staring at my open books. I have no ambition to study and no desire to go downstairs and play video games with the guys. Instead, I hold onto my phone and stare at it like it's some foreign object. I've been debating with myself for the last ten minutes on whether I should text Lucy or not.

Ah, fuck it. Here goes nothing.

> Me: Hey Lucy. Just checking to see what you're up to right now?

> Me: Would you want to come over here and study with me?

It feels like I hold my breath for five minutes but it's probably only ten seconds when she responds back.

> Lucy: Yeah, I can do that. Give me 15 minutes.

Suddenly, I'm sweating with nerves that she's going to be coming over here in less than fifteen minutes. I jump out of bed, tossing the phone on my desk and quickly trying to tidy the place up. The bedroom I share is fairly cramped because both Killer and I have full-size beds that take up most of the space. We share the dresser, although technically it's mine cause I'm the only one who uses it. Killian just throws his stuff on the floor of the small closet. We also share a desk that's piled high with books and papers, and I do a double take when I run my eye over the stacks contents.

Oh shit, is that a partially eaten sandwich?

I quickly dispose of the unwanted items and make my bed, giving the room one last look before I go into the bathroom to check my reflection in the mirror. My hair is still damp, so it looks darker than my normal sandy blond color, and I haven't shaved in two days so there's a light crop of stubble over my jawline. I rub a hand over the stubble and decide to keep it, but I do add a splash of cologne just to be presentable.

We're just going to study.

Taking the stairs two by two, I let the guys know that Lucy is coming over and that they better be on their best behavior and not talk shit. They all let out a collective laugh. Then I point two fingers from my eyes to Killian's and back to mine, giving him the signal of *stay the fuck out of our room.* He grins and gives me a thumbs-up in agreement.

I'm pulling out two bottles of water from the fridge when there's a knock on the door.

I hold the bottles in one hand and rush to open it, finding Lucy on the threshold of the porch looking both shy and sexy as fuck.

Who the hell am I kidding? I'm not getting any studying done tonight.

Chapter Eighteen

L ucy

Why am I doing my hair? Why bother with mascara? I keep telling myself it's just in case Hendy is around.

Yes, that's why. It definitely has nothing to do with the hot-as-hell wide receiver that I'm tutoring. Emmett is just my friend.

"Friend zone," I repeat quietly to myself as I look in the mirror one last time and give myself a mental thumbs-up.

I step out of the bathroom and Kelsie whistles. "Damn! Hot date?"

"Nope. I mean, not really. I'm just going over there to study," I stammer.

"*Right,*" she says, drawing out the last syllable with a look that clearly says she doesn't believe me. I hadn't wanted to tell them what happened the other night but they forced it out of me. I'm not too proud to admit that I opened up like a bag of candy, spilling all the deets about Emmett's skills in the bedroom.

"I'll see you later," I say as I grab my things. My face heats and flames red as I head over to Emmett's house, wondering if we'll talk about what happened Saturday night.

The fall wind is wicked today and I wrap my coat tighter to my chest, pulling the lapels up around my neck. I walk faster and manage to get there in record time.

I stand on the front step way too long before knocking. What am I doing here? I knock lightly, hoping they didn't hear it, and take a step back, as if by doing so I can take back the sound my fist just made against the door. But then it opens and Emmett is standing there, smiling warmly at me, and I forget how to breathe for a moment.

"Hey," he says softly.

"Hi," I reply awkwardly, shuffling my weight from one foot to another.

"Get in here. It's cold outside." He motions for me to step through the threshold into the house. I hesitate for half a second before entering. I can hear the laughter of men in another room, and what sounds like a video game involving sports as the cheering of a crowd can be heard above the banter amongst the players. I rub my arms to warm them through my coat—or maybe to calm my nerves. The door clicks closed and then Emmett's large body is behind mine. He wraps his arms around my body, locking my arms against my sides, as if this is all a normal greeting.

"You're cold, babe. Let's get you warmed up," he whispers against my ear. I shiver, but not from the cold. He called me babe. No one has ever called me that before.

It's just pretend.

His hands stroke up and down my arms and then he

takes my hands in his and brings them to his face. He leans forward, gazing at me intensely, and blows hot air against them. Holy shitballs! I feel my body responding as a throbbing sensation begins between my legs.

"Better?" he whispers after a moment, catching and holding my gaze. I nod, too afraid to speak because this seemingly nonsexual action has left me breathless.

"Good. I made us hot chocolate," he says proudly as he steers me toward the kitchen where mismatched mugs have piles of whipped cream on top.

"Wow, look at you, pulling out all the barista stops." I want to add how sweet I think it is but I keep that to myself.

He chuckles, handing me one and picking up the other. "Here's to getting some serious studying done." He raises his mug and clinks it against mine.

"Uh, right. Cheers," I murmur as I take a sip and moan at how good it tastes. Shit. Why is that so hot? And I'm not referring to the hot chocolate. It's the way his darkened eyes watch me intently that makes me warm inside.

"What?"

"You have a little something, right here," he says, his thumb wiping away whipped cream from my upper lip. I swipe the tip of my tongue over the spot he just touched and stare at him as he slides his thumb in his mouth and sucks the cream away. If my panties weren't wet before, they certainly are now.

I swallow hard. "S-should we go s-study?" I ask, trying to form the words that come out as a stuttered mess.

He smirks and raises his eyebrow. "Study?"

I clear my throat. "Yeah...study."

"Come on. I kicked Killer out of our room so we could have some peace and quiet. Everyone's busy with this PS5 tournament that Hendy made up," he explains as he takes my free hand and begins walking. I pause at the entrance to the family room where eight rowdy guys are huddled around a giant television screen. Two of them have controllers in hand. Hendy's watching intently but glances in my direction and smiles.

"Hey, Lucy, what's up?"

I feel a goofy grin spread across my face because OMG, he knows my name now! This whole ruse has actually worked.

"Hey, Joel. Just here to study."

He shrugs. "Cool. Do you play?" he asks, motioning to the screen.

I check out the football video game and shake my head.

"Bummer. I was going to get you to join my team. Guess we'll have to find another game to play," he says with a wink.

Holy moly guacamole. Is Hendy flirting with me now? No fucking way!

A tight squeeze of my palm reminds me I'm here with Emmett. *Oops.*

"We have a lot of studying to do. See you guys later," Emmett growls.

A few of the players lift their heads and nod, barely registering my presence because they are so sucked into the video game.

"Later, boys," I call out, making eye contact again with Hendy. He licks his lips and then smiles at me again.

I almost forgot how attractive he is when he smiles. I used to study that smile like it was a cure for a disease. I would imagine it focused on me as I lay in bed at night, wondering what it would be like to have Joel's attention. And now that I do, the intensity of my interest has faded.

Like a piece of bubble gum. It's super sweet when you first taste it, but the flavor goes away quickly.

But I'm still giddy when I'm around Emmett, who I follow up the stairs.

I shift my gaze upwards and find Emmett's ass is in my direct line of sight as he leads me up the stairs. He really does have a perfectly solid ass. I even got to touch it the other night and can confirm it also feels pretty perfect.

I shake my head to clear the thoughts it shouldn't have. Emmett leads me to a room and opens the door. I look around, surprised to find the room is so clean. Even Emmett's bed is made.

Or what I assume is Emmett's bed because the other one has magazines about agriculture on the nightstand and a shirt that says "Cowboys do it best" lying at the foot of it.

I press my lips together to keep from giggling.

"Here, let me take your coat," Emmett says as he steps in behind me. I can feel the brush of his chest against my back. Why do I like that so much? I realize I feel safe with Emmett behind me.

I undo the buttons and he pulls it down my arms as I slip out of it before he lays it over his desk chair. He motions for me to take a seat on the bed. I set my bag down and sit. Then I open my bag and extract some note cards from the pocket, placing them on his bed. He lifts a brow, turning the chair around to sit in front of me, some books in his lap, but remains silent.

I finish my hot chocolate and he reaches a hand out to take the mug. Our fingers touch as he lifts the mug out of my grasp. My nerves have me trembling under his touch. It's just a study session, I tell myself. He sets it down on the nightstand and then sets his mug down next to it. When he looks back at me, his eyes crinkle with a smile and he leans forward.

"You have cream on your lip again." He motions to my upper lip.

"I do?"

He nods. I reach up and wipe it from my lip, but before I can lick it off, he grabs my hand and looks at me for a long moment, slowly inching our joined hands to his mouth. His eyes stay locked on mine as his tongue swipes the white cream off my index finger and then slips it between his lips, sucking it between his teeth.

And it's official. My panties burst into flames. I clench my thighs in response to this erotic gesture. Why does Emmett make my body react like this?

"We never finished our lesson the other day," he says in a low gravelly voice.

I swallow and shake my head in agreement.

"Shall we finish it now?" His hooded eyes look at me, waiting for my consent.

Why does that make this ten times sexier? He's letting me decide. He's giving me the choice, but right now, I don't want to make decisions. I want his tongue and fingers on me and in me. I want Emmett to make me forget my name, my major, and my end-goal of being with his teammate.

I don't reply, I simply react. I shove the notecards onto the floor and they go fluttering in every direction like little three-by-five snowflakes. And then I straddle Emmett's lap and wrap my arms around his neck.

His eyes widen a little in shock at my brazen behavior and I smirk as I lean forward, enjoying the power I feel over this huge, sexy guy. "I'm ready for my next lesson, professor," I whisper against his ear.

He places a hand on my jaw and tilts my head as he

presses his lips to mine. As he slides his tongue along my lips, I forget about my goal to be with Hendy. I forget about school. I forget about everything but Emmett. He kisses me like it's his only job in the world. He kisses me like nothing else matters but me. My body begins to involuntarily grind against his.

I'm barely aware of my movements until a low growl reverberates from Emmett's throat and I'm suddenly in his hold, being hoisted in the air before laid out on the bed beneath him. I automatically spread my legs as he presses his hips down, his erection pressing hard against my lower belly. A small moan escapes my lips.

"Yes to the skirt. No to these tights," he grumbles. His hands work the fabric down over my hips before hiking up my skirt to gain better access.

I giggle. "It was cold out."

"You won't be cold now. I promise you that." He tugs the hem of my skirt and pushes it up past my belly, then yanks my tights and panties down to pull my legs free and throws all of the offending articles of clothing on his floor.

"I'm telling you, babe. Anything that stops a man from getting to this sweet end zone is an obstacle and we don't like it," he snickers disapprovingly as he licks my lower lip. His eyes focus on the apex of my legs. "Much better."

We kiss and touch and make out for long minutes—maybe even hours. It's hard to tell time when his hands and mouth explore every part they can reach. My own hands begin their tentative movement over, and then under the material of his shirt, loving the way his muscles tense and his breath hitches when I trace over the rounds of his nipples or down the center of his torso.

Finally, after what seems forever, our bodies eagerly

awaiting more, he lifts his eyes to mine, regarding me hungrily. A curse escapes under his breath.

"I need this gone."

"Huh?" I ask, still dazed from our kisses. Before I can ask more, Emmett begins fumbling with the zipper of my skirt, tugging it down. It gets stuck until I lift my hips up to remove it. Then, he quickly takes off my top and bra, leaving me completely naked.

I glance down at my nakedness and snort. "Well, this doesn't seem quite fair."

Emmett chuckles and reaches behind his neck to grab the back of his T-shirt. I watch as he does that one-handed removal thing with his shirt, pulling it slowly over his head. Why do guys do that? And why is it so damn hot?

He quickly stands and removes his boxers, jeans, and socks.

"Better?" he smirks, crawling back onto the bed and settling himself between my legs.

I take a moment to take in all of him, glancing nervously at his large cock he's taken into his hand. I was right. He is way bigger than my high school boyfriend.

"Don't worry, Lucy. We're going to take our time today. I want this lesson to be good for you," he says quietly as he runs his lips across my jawline.

"Okay," I manage as I release a long breath, trying to calm my nerves.

When his lips finally touch mine, I forget all about my nerves. He strokes his tongue alongside mine, taking away any thoughts I have about the note cards that are now completely out of order on his floor.

"What about Killer?" I whisper as he trails kisses down to my breasts.

"I told him to fuck off because we had serious studying

to do. No interruptions today," he adds as his lips close around my right nipple. I groan at the intense sensation that radiates to my core.

He braces himself on one elbow while his free hand reaches between my legs and his fingers part my folds. I can feel how slick I am as he runs two fingers back and forth through my wetness.

He makes a guttural sound and his lips pop free from my nipple.

"Jesus, Lucy, you are so wet," he murmurs reverently as he continues kissing down my belly while slowly sliding his fingers inside me, first one and then a second. My hips thrust up to meet their movements as they glide in and out.

He presses a kiss against my lower abdomen and I find myself squirming. I want his lips and tongue on me elsewhere.

"Patience. You deserve to be worshiped. If a guy isn't doing that, he doesn't deserve you," he says, casting a meaningful glance up at me.

What guy is he talking about? Does he mean Joel? Or just any guy in general? At this point, I couldn't care less about Joel.

Our heated gazes lock. His lips cover my clit and he sucks hard as he curls his fingers inside me. After only one time, he knows what I need. It's like he read my manual once and now he knows how everything operates on my body.

"Oh God...don't stop," I beg as my head falls onto the pillow and my eyes roll back in my head. He doubles his efforts. My hips start thrusting against his face and fingers. I need more, so much more.

My fingers wrap around his sheets, and I grip them as if they can keep me from floating away. I feel him slide a third finger inside me and then I come hard. I try to stay quiet, but a low moan escapes. I slap a hand over my mouth as I slowly come down from my high.

My eyes stay shut as I feel Emmett move up my body, trailing kisses along the way. He reaches over to his nightstand and I hear the rip of a foil packet. My eyes open and I watch him roll the condom over his length. He fists himself again before sliding his erection through my folds. I'm so wet that he glides easily up and down.

"Are you sure, Lucy? We can stop this lesson whenever you want," he asks as I feel the head of his dick lodge against my opening.

I nod. I want this. I have wanted this for days now. It's just a lesson, just for fun, right? I decide not to overthink it. "Yes," I murmur as he slowly sinks into me, one glorious inch at a time.

His girth makes it sting a little, but as he pulls out and slips back inside, coating his length with my wetness, the slight pain is replaced with my desire, my need to have us joined together as closely as humanly possible.

For this one moment, I'm going to stop thinking about my goal of being with Hendy, and just enjoy everything Emmett is offering. After all, none of this is real, right? This is just an extra bonus out of our fake relationship.

Yeah, I'm sure that's all it is.

Even though the feel of Emmett buried deep inside me feels anything but fake.

Chapter Nineteen

E^{mmett}

Fucking hell. Lucy is driving me to the edge of orgasm faster than a girl has ever done before.

Maybe it's all the time I've spent getting to know her over the last month and the friendship we've developed. I found this different side of Lucy that I hadn't expected when we first met.

She's loosened up around me. Maybe she doesn't have as much to prove to me or to herself anymore. It's still annoying as hell the way she looks at Hendy, blushing under his compliments and from his smiles. But I guess the proof is in the evidence. She's here with me in my bed right now and not him.

And thank God for that.

My hands bracket each side of her slim shoulders as I stare down into her beautiful face. With each thrust of my hips, her lips part with a pleasured "O" shape and her eyes close in pleasure and I can't help what pops out of my mouth.

"God, you're so beautiful."

Lucy's eyes snap open seemingly taking in the veracity of my statement. Then she turns her head to the side as if embarrassed by my affection. I place my thumb underneath her chin and draw her eyes back to mine.

"Don't do that, Luce. You. Are. Beautiful."

A slow, sexy smile turns up at the corners of her mouth and then she bites down on her lip just as I lean down and suck that lip between my teeth. The kiss turns scorching-hot as I sweep my tongue inside. A hungry groan rips free from deep within my chest when she sucks my tongue hard.

A sharp shock of electricity ricochets from my balls up my spine and I know I'm getting close to letting it all go. I bend down and flick the tip of my tongue over one of her nipples as she shutters in pleasure.

"You like that?" I ask, my voice breathless and tight.

She responds with a breathy answer herself. "Oh, yeah, so much."

I roll my hips experimentally, my cock hitting a deep place within her, extricating a low moan from her throat.

"And how about that?"

This time her response is to curl her fingers around the back of my shoulder blades and dig her heels into the backs of my thighs.

An urgent, fervent need to make sure she finds her release first quickly overtakes me.

Pressing myself up with an extended elbow, I use my other hand to reach between us, slipping my finger through the wet entrance where we are joined.

Lucy sucks in a harsh breath and I swallow it with my

kiss. I continue to make rapid, shallow thrusts as my thumb makes tiny circles over her clit. Her nails dig into my skin and my body comes alive with a greedy need to empty my throbbing cock inside her.

And then, with one more circular motion of my hips, her hips buck up and she lets out a long full moan.

Within seconds I follow her over the edge, my entire body shaking in the aftershock of the orgasm that tears through me.

I practically sag on top of her, my arms giving out as I drop my head against the pillow at her cheek. The rhythm of our breathing is in sync as contentment steals over me.

I'm so lost in her sweet scent and the warmth of her neck that I forget I'm practically crushing her until she pushes with a palm against my chest.

"Emmett, I can't breathe," she says with a soft giggle and I scramble to move.

I pull out, pinching at the condom before rolling to my side. I toss the used rubber in the trash and return to stare at her profile, lifting to run a finger over her jawline. A stray piece of hair has broken loose from her now messy hairdo and I tuck it behind her ear.

"How's that?" I ask quietly, a trace of humor in my voice. "Was that a lesson worth learning?"

Lucy turns her face and stares into my eyes, a slow smile spreading across her full lips. She lifts a hand and cradles my cheek, her fingertips gliding over my day-old scruff.

And then she blows me away with what she says next.

"I think that is a lesson I might need some more practice with," she teases, rolling the tip of her tongue over her lip. "But there might be another assignment I need some help with, if you're willing to give extra credit."

I give her a suspicious look. "And what's that?"

A deep blush creeps up over her neck making her look both sexy and vulnerable at the same time. She lifts her shoulder in a slight shrug.

"Blow jobs."

* * *

The campus is quiet when I finally walk Lucy back the few blocks from my house to her dorm. I hold her hand in mine as we silently make our way across the quad.

It's a little after two in the morning, and I know once I get home I'm going to sleep like the dead after the night we had together.

To say we were insatiable is an understatement. Once we got started, there was no stopping those "lessons" to be learned. And let me tell you, Lucy is a great student: eager, willing, and sexy as fuck. Even I learned a thing or two tonight. Like how to take my time.

When she got down on her knees between my legs I thought I might just black out, I was so turned on by the sight. She was tentative at first, but once I gave her some ideas on what I liked and suggested that my dick wasn't breakable, she got into it with the excitement of a novice. She'd admitted to me that she had only given head once before and said it had been a disaster. If that's the truth, then she is a quick learner. Within a few minutes she had me coming down her throat.

And now, as the darkness envelops us and the quiet hum of the campus surrounds us, it feels like we're the only two people in the world who are awake. It brings a strange new awareness between us, like an electric sizzle from downed power lines or something. Whatever it is, its inten-

145

sity shocks me. Does Lucy feel it? Or is it just me reacting to the intimacy we shared tonight?

We make our way to the stoop at the entrance of her building and I squeeze her hand.

"So..." I hesitate and look down into her eyes blinking with uncertainty. "I guess this is where I leave you."

She bends her head and stares between our feet, swaying from one foot to the other. "Yeah, guess so."

I'm at a loss for words. Clearly feeling something big but unable to express it properly. I've never felt this way about a girl before but I don't know what to do about it.

Instead of opening this box of questions and letting her know what I feel about us, I go with casual and skip the thoughts inside my head.

"I have a busy week ahead of me, so I probably won't see you until we leave on Saturday morning for the ski trip."

"Okay," she says softly. "That's fine. I understand."

Ah, fuck this shit.

I lift my hands and cup her cheeks, her eyes blinking in surprise at my sudden movement as I crash my mouth against hers, kissing her and hoping to chase away the doubts she has in her head. Even though this was only supposed to be pretend, everything I'm feeling inside is very real.

"Lucy, this thing is..." I try to find the words to explain to her what she means to me when suddenly the door bursts open and three girls walk out, all giggling and stumbling everywhere and running into each other like they're circus clowns. When they see us standing there, they realize what they've done and there's a chorus of *oohs* and *aahs*.

"Oopsie! Sorry to interrupt, *Luuucy!*" slurs one of them, her hand flying to her mouth as her eyes bounce and roll between me and Lucy and then go wide in recognition at who I am. "Whoa...EJ. Didn't mean to cockblock you, bro."

They laugh some more and begin to walk away as I throw my arm around Lucy's shoulder and tug her into my chest before they knock her over on their way to the quad.

"Well, that was sure entertaining." I chuckle and kiss the top of her head as Lucy

pulls away and searches her bag for her ID to re-open the door.

She looks at me one more time and smiles. "Thanks for a fun study session. I'll see you Saturday morning."

And with that, she opens the door and walks inside, leaving me standing alone as I stare after her, wondering how I've gotten myself into this mess.

And how I plan to get myself out of it with my heart intact.

Chapter Twenty

L^{ucy}

I freeze, staring in terror at what's above me.

The mountain looms overhead, but I can't even see the peak with all the clouds in the way. Emmett and the guys were all excited over an impending snow storm as we drove up here. Apparently, they are stoked about the "fresh powder."

"So, should I call my family to say goodbye now or just before you give me the ski lesson?" I joke, my eyes still fixed on the snowy paths I can see down the mountainside. Swallowing, I envision my potential untimely death via ski accident.

Emmett laughs and puts an arm around my shoulders. Out of the corner of my eye, I see Hendy watching us, which means Emmett's obviously putting on a show for his benefit. I turn and face him to play along.

Only, Emmett's face doesn't look like he's simply playing. But I should know by now that my fake boyfriend is a really convincing actor.

He runs a gloved finger over my cheek. "I promise I won't let anything happen to you, baby."

I shiver under his touch and his sweet term of endearment. But then a look of concern washes over his features.

"Are you cold? Let's get you inside and warmed up," he says, abruptly turning to walk us up the front steps of the cabin. Apparently, it belongs to Hendy's aunt and uncle and they offered it up to him for this annual weekend trip. Emmett said this is the first time anyone has brought a date along as it's been a guys only trip in the past.

Emmett opens the door and I take a moment to look around. Hendy is already hauling a second load of bags out of the back of his Jeep.

"You guys want to take the second master suite on this floor?" Hendy asks as he enters behind us, bringing with him a blast of cold air. "Down at the far end of the house so we don't have to listen to EJ's sex noises."

I glance in his direction, my eyes the size of donuts and cheeks heating like someone just turned on a sauna. "There's more than one master suite?"

Hendy's puffy ski jacket makes a crinkling sound as he sets down the bags. He looks like a cross between a lumberjack and an Olympic skier with his beard growth and high-end parka. Hendy is most definitely hot. I take a deep breath.

This weekend could change everything.

This play-pretend farce with Emmett will come to an end this weekend, leaving me available to date Joel.

I swallow down the confusion that seems to be lodged in my throat.

"There are two suites with bathrooms down here and two more upstairs, plus two other bedrooms that share a bathroom. I have three cousins and we have all been coming up here with friends and family for years. My aunt and uncle are loaded." Hendy explains, matter-of-fact as he carries his bag toward the back. He motions for us to follow him.

I take in the exposed wood beams and the cozy rug in front of a giant stone fireplace that climbs all the way up the wall to the vaulted ceiling. The kitchen is state-of-the-art with stainless steel appliances and stone countertops. The island has six bar stools. A giant round table is in the far corner of the space with ten chairs around it. This house is gorgeous and huge, like the homes I see on television or in movies.

Hendy leads us down the hallway and we pass a guest half-bath and laundry room and mudroom with access outside. Finally, we reach the end. One doorway is to the left, and another farther down seems to open off a hall alcove and leads to a giant bedroom.

"That's the guest suite." Hendy motions in the direction of the one on the left with an open door. "I'll be over in this one." He walks under the arched entry into the suite that must be his aunt and uncle's bedroom because it is even bigger than the one we're in front of.

Emmett presses a hand to my lower back, guiding me inside our room. I plop my bag down on the bed and stare at the opulence of the suite.

"It's confirmed," I say as I walk over to the open door of the bathroom. "This bathroom is indeed larger than my dorm room." I swing my arms out wide. "Holy hell, this place is incredible. I've never stayed in a place this nice. I wish we'd snuck Grace and Kelsie up here. This walk-in closet could have doubled as another bedroom."

Emmett laughs. "Yeah, Hendy's uncle owns a cement company and his aunt is a marketing executive. They definitely didn't skimp on this property."

I walk in to take a look at the enormous walk-in shower. It has a literal seat—a full *bench*—four different shower heads, and a bunch of buttons on the wall.

"That looks...intense," I say as I feel Emmett walk up behind me. I glance to my right and catch us in the vanity mirror as he wraps his arms around my waist. His body towers over mine. He drops his chin to the top of my head, leaning down a bit to do so, then follows my gaze and smiles at our reflection.

"What?"

"Shower sex is so much better when you can watch." His grin morphs into a sexy smirk.

I feel my cheeks turn pink under the implication of his comment and I'm about to tell him I've never done anything like that when he spins me around to face him.

"Shall we have a lesson later?" he asks with hooded eyes.

I bite my lip as the blush creeps lower and expands down my neck, and I begin to tingle between my legs because damn that would be hot. I don't trust my voice so I just nod enthusiastically. Why is the idea of shower sex so appealing? I envision the water cascading down Emmett's body.

"But first, let's get you a ski lesson." He kisses the tip of my nose and then swats my butt playfully. Shit, I should not have been daydreaming of shower sex with Emmett. Now, I have no desire to learn to ski. I'd rather stay here and have my first shower sex lesson.

I release a whoop of laughter, jumping out of his hold. I immediately miss his warmth. It is freezing up here, and I suddenly have the urge to stay in this bathroom with Emmett and try out the over-the-top shower instead of put on ski pants and fall flat on my ass on the bunny hill.

"Promise you won't kill me?"

"I promise. But first things first. We need to get you into some warmer clothes." I begrudgingly nod and head to my bag to pile on the layers.

Fifteen minutes later, I'm bundled up and feel like the kid in *A Christmas Story*.

"I'm not sure how I'm going to ski with all these clothes on," I note as I trudge to the front door, flapping my arms experimentally. Maybe I can just roll down the hill.

Emmett smiles. "Trust me. I think we can figure it out."

He pauses and glances around the house at the everyone who just arrived. "Hey, guys, I'm taking Lucy to the bunny hill for her first ski lesson. See you out there."

Various people yell "bye" and "have fun" and "don't kill Lucy," which doesn't make me feel any better. The shower sounds even better, but I don't think I can bend my legs enough to get back up the front porch steps.

Emmett drives us to the main lodge in Hendy's big rig. Apparently, for those who know what they are doing, they can literally walk out the back door of the cabin, down a trail, and take off skiing down the mountainside. But for the bunny hill, it's easier to drive around the corner, park at the resort, and take a chairlift up.

The bunny hill looks far bigger than Emmett told me it would. At least adolescent rabbit size. I'm by far the oldest person out here. An instructor is teaching a small class of kids on one side. Some look no older than four years old.

Some are wearing skis and with whom I assume are their parents, and some of the kids are strapped to snowboards. They all look so cute in their snow gear, helmets, and goggles. One little kid even has a helmet with a blue Mohawk sticking out of it. And then there is a small group of teenagers trying to help a friend who has fallen over on her ass and can't stop laughing long enough to stand up.

I swallow as I give Emmett a pointed look.

"That is going to be me in a matter of minutes."

How is it that I never learned how to ski? I mean, I don't live that far away from here. Emmett chuckles but doesn't question my inexperience, doesn't even tease me about having to use the bunny hill. He just patiently begins explaining the basics to me, helping me into skis, strapping the bindings, and handing me the poles.

"Try to point the skis like this," he suggests, demonstrating the action. "That will help you slow down and stop."

I try to copy his stance but my skis get crossed at the tips and I wobble. He smiles, grabbing my waist to keep me from the same fate as that girl, and bends down to untangle the skis. Even with three layers on, I can feel the heat of his hand, and it's doing things to my lady parts that it shouldn't be doing. Why does Emmett have this effect on me? I shake that thought from my head as I try to listen to what he's telling me.

He slides around me like a professional. "Let's do this. We are going to take that little conveyor belt looking thing over there up to the first stop. And then we'll go down together for the first time."

"Okay," I squeak, nerves contracting my vocal cords. Emmett comes up behind me as we ride up what really does feel like a conveyor belt. I'm sure it has some official name but I'm glad Emmett is using layman terms so I can understand because this skiing thing is way outside my academic comfort zone.

I feel his arms come around me and he easily lifts me and sets me down at our stop.

"Put your skis together. I'm going to put mine on the outside, and I'll hold on to you as we go down. Just tuck your poles against your sides, alright?"

I press my lips together and swallow nervously before nodding my understanding. Emmett gets us in position and as soon as his strong arms are wrapped around my center, I suddenly feel calmer.

He leans forward so his hot breath is next to my earlobe underneath my helmet. "I got you, Lucy. I won't let anything happen to you."

He squeezes me a little for reassurance. I turn my head and look up at him. "I trust you," I whisper.

"Good. Let's get you skiing." He pushes off and we start moving forward, guiding me with words to bend my knees and lean in different directions.

It's not so bad. The hill seems less daunting when you're on it. And even less so when you have a giant wide receiver's arms wrapped around your waist.

I start to relax and squeal with delight as we make a slight turn in the snow. Emmett chuckles and something about this moment of pure happiness hits me square in the chest.

I like Emmett Hudson.

I really *like* him. I suddenly feel a little strange. Do I have a crush on Emmett? How is it possible if I have a crush on Hendy? Hendy's my goal. I need to stay focused.

Sure, I have these feelings about Emmett, but that's because...maybe because the sex was so good.

Yes, that has to be it.

I'll just have one last lesson with him and enjoy today, and then we really should get on with our fake breakup before I become any more confused.

I'm concentrating so hard on what needs to happen this weekend that I'm not focused on what I'm doing. It's then that I feel my ski slide over an icy patch and we're falling. Emmett leans backwards at the last minute and I land right on top of him.

"Are you okay?" he asks, keeping a hand wrapped securely around my waist.

"I think so. But damn, this ice is slippery. They should have slippery when wet signs here," I say and then clamp my hand over my mouth when I realize what I just implied.

Emmett starts laughing as he helps me back up on my skis and gets me upright.

"I know something else that's slippery when wet," he replies with a wink.

"Maybe we should go have another lesson off the slopes," I say as I bat my eyelashes.

"Good try, but we came out to ski. We need to finish what we started and have time for that other lesson later."

I'm surprised he doesn't just jump for joy over my suggestion of sex and it stings a little. But he's right, I did come out here to learn how to ski, and after putting on way too many layers of clothes, so we might as well finish the ski lesson first.

As we take a few more runs and I finally do one on my own, Emmett's excitement over my success has me deciding to wait to discuss our fake breakup till later. I'm having too much fun with him to kill the mood.

"You got this, Lucy. We'll have you skiing down the big trails in no time," he assures me. I take his outstretched hand, realizing that I'm going to miss moments like this when we end things.

I just hope I don't lose Emmett's friendship in the process.

Chapter Twenty-One

Emmett

After an agonizing two hours out on the slopes—where I had a hard-on the entire time under my long underwear and ski pants, making it very difficult to move—we finally made our way down the ski slope slowly but surely and decided to call it a day.

Even with all the layers of winter wear, holding her as I taught her ski techniques had my body amped up from the beginning. Now that we're back in the house, I feel like I could go from zero to sixty in no time at all. I want to skip all the pretense and take her back to the bedroom and forget the outside world.

Yet I hesitate in making the next move. I don't want Lucy to be uncomfortable since we are still technically only pretending to date and we're not a real couple behind closed doors. But it feels bigger than that now. There's something between us but I don't know what to do about it or how to bring it up with her.

We take off our boots and outerwear at the side door and hang them to dry in the mudroom, then grab some waters from the fridge and head back into the bedroom.

I lean against the door, closing it behind us, and watch Lucy take off her sweater and long-sleeved shirt, placing it on the bed. With her back to me, I notice the gentle curves of her waist, the smooth skin of her back, and her ass that seems to taunt me to do something.

I'm ready to tell her that we should have our break-up scene tonight in front of everyone when Lucy turns around, her eyes glazing over with what looks like lust.

We stare at each other, each of us unmoving, as something stronger than a magnetic force field seems to pull us toward one another.

When she stops a few inches in front of where I stand, she surprises the fuck out of me by removing her bra, so she is left in only her leggings.

I quirk an interested eyebrow and casually lean my shoulder against the back of the door. My hungry gaze sweeps over her as I strain to keep my hands to myself.

"What are you thinking about?"

She glances toward the bathroom and then back to me, chewing on that delectable bottom lip again.

She extends her hand to me and slips her fingers through mine and tugs me to follow behind her.

"I'm thinking about that shower and that next lesson you promised me."

My dick jumps for joy, and as if sensing this, she turns back and glances down between my legs, a sly smile hooking up the corners of her mouth.

I give her a shrug of my shoulders. "I could go for a shower."

We walk into the expansive bathroom, our feet quietly padding across the heated marble flooring.

We stop in front of the shower door and I open it, turning on the faucet to let the water warm up. Spinning back to Lucy, I find her wiggling out of her leggings, the skin of her thighs dotted with goose bumps.

"Come here and let me warm you up," I say, extending my hand for her to walk toward me.

"I like where this is heading."

Lucy's bare breasts are on display, their sweet plumpness turning me into a salivating, eager mess. I groan in anticipation. Reaching out, I pluck a distended nipple between my thumb and index finger. Lucy's moan sends a shooting pleasure down my spine and coursing straight to my groin.

I curl an arm around her bare waist and tuck her into me, continuing to massage her firm breasts in my hands as her head drops back in pleasure.

Bending over just slightly, I flick my tongue over the hardened peak of her nipple, taking the first taste of her in my mouth since last weekend. She's both salty and sweet and the best thing I've ever tasted. I open wider and suck more of her into my mouth, rolling my tongue over her delicious skin.

"I've fucking dreamed about this," I murmur against her breast, moving to the other side and taking another nipple into my mouth while covering her bare breast in my hand and massaging gently.

Lucy wraps one hand around the back of my neck and her other hand drops to my ass, squeezing my cheek roughly.

"Me too."

I quickly divest us both of our remaining clothes and we make our way into the shower stall, now enclosed by the steamed-up glass partition. Once we're both wet, I reach for the lemon-scented body wash and pour some in my hand, lathering it up before returning my hands to her sensitive breasts. I continue my seduction by caressing and rubbing the soapy gel over every inch of her body. Before I reach the juncture between her legs, I turn her around to face the marbled wall, placing her hands against the cold tile surface. Then I move my hands in front of her, gently gliding them over her stomach and down her inner thighs until one finger reaches the warmth at her entrance.

"I think this area needs a little attention, don't you?"

Lucy lets out a sharp gasp as I simultaneously press my rigid length against her lower back and slide my finger through her folds. She twists her head to the side to meet my mouth, her tongue greeting mine in an erotic welcome as I capture her lips in a hot, demanding kiss.

My finger moves in a circular motion over her sensitive nub as she pants out short, punctuated words in a shaky breath.

"Oh God... yes... right... *there*...."

I smile against the warm wet skin of her neck, teasing at her entrance with my finger until I thrust inside, using my thumb to continue drawing out her orgasm.

I can tell she's getting close as her legs begin to shake, her body tightening against me. My eyes flick upwards to the handheld shower head and I decide to bring out the big guns.

I remove my fingers from her sensitive flesh, hot and swollen with need, and I reach for the shower head, pulling it down from its hook and bringing it between her legs.

My voice is rough and low when I whisper in her ear. "Confession time. Have you ever done this by yourself?"

She gasps out a little hiccup and shakes her head, her wet hair falling over her shoulder. "No."

"Good. This will be your next lesson."

My ramrod cock wedges in the seam of her ass. I use my foot to kick at her heels and open her stance wider, holding her up with my arm around her middle and position the shower head at her core feeling the vibrations ricochet through her body. The strong current of water seems to rock her world as she cries out, her hands wildly straining to hold on to something. Lucy throws a hand behind my neck, digging her nails into my skin with the intensity of her climax.

The moment she goes limp against my chest, I turn off the water and she heaves out a sigh.

Her voice is breathy as she stammers, "Oh my God, Emmett. Best. Lesson. So Far."

I chuckle against her neck. "I'd have to agree because I think the rest of the house heard that too."

She turns in my arms, clutching on to me so she doesn't fall, and her eyes grow to the size of saucers. "Are you serious? Was I that loud?" She lays her forehead against my bare chest. "I'm going to die of embarrassment."

I chuckle, reaching out to grab a towel hanging from the hook on the wall and wrap it around her. "Well, I won't. I'm going to look like a fucking king for making my girl so happy that she screams when I make her come."

Lucy smacks at my bicep and sticks her tongue out at me. "Gah. You're terrible."

"Nah...I'd say I'm pretty damn good," I retort with a chuckle.

I follow her out and step onto the mat to dry off. She

reaches forward to grab a brush and brushes the wet, tangled hair out of her face. I place a kiss on her forehead, breathing in her lemon-scented skin. My lips move down her jawline. When I land on her lips, I cover her mouth with mine, the brush dropping from her hand and clattering to the floor.

I pull away and find her eyes staring up at me, still hazy with desire. And then, without warning, Lucy's hand drops to my cock, wrapping it with her fist and slowly stroking the length the way she knows I like. Fuck, she's a good student.

"I need you inside me, Emmett. Now." She arches her brow and tugs me towards the bedroom.

I'm not about to argue with her demand and I follow behind like a needy puppy, ready to pounce.

Chapter Twenty-Two

L ucy

The logical part of my brain questions whether this is still part of our shower "lesson" and the rest of my brain screams "screw the lesson." I want Emmett and if he wants to give that to me, then I won't protest.

When we make it to the bedroom, I give Emmett a little shove and he falls onto the bed with a soft *thwomp*. He reaches out and pulls me down on top of him, towels discarded so our naked bodies press together in all the right places.

My eyes widen. I've never really been the take-charge type of woman in a sexual relationship—not that I've had a lot of sexual relationships to speak of. Which is exactly why I've been taking notes—figuratively, of course—during every lesson with Emmett so I can put them to use at a later time.

Oddly enough, being with someone else that isn't Emmett doesn't even sound appealing to me anymore.

What *is* appealing is a naked Emmett underneath me.

As if thinking I've stalled because of my nerves, Emmett reaches over and pulls a condom out of his bag next to the bed. He turns my palm up and places it in my hand.

"You're in charge," he says as his eyes rove over my body. "Do your worst."

I lift an eyebrow and stare down at the perfection that is Emmett Hudson. How did I get so lucky to have such a hot boyfriend? I mean, *fake* boyfriend?

Emmett flexes his hips and his erection strains hotly against my core, bringing me out of my head. That need I felt in the shower surges back to life and I make quick work of rolling the condom down his length. He keeps his hands on my thighs, drawing small circles on the insides of them, teasing me but never quite touching where I need him to. I give a growl of dissatisfaction.

I lean up and take him in my hand, positioning him at my opening before slowly sinking down onto him. My eyes close at the fullness inside me. I sigh in pleasure as I allow myself to adjust to his size. It's when I feel his hands grip my hips that I open my eyes and find him staring intently up at me.

"You're killing me," he whispers, bumping his pelvis up, his cock going even deeper.

I bite my lip, placing my hands over his pecs, pushing myself up and then slamming my body back down. The relief is so intense it nearly breaks me. His fingers flex against my skin and, as if in response to my unspoken pleas, he lets out a harsh breath and moves inside me.

Suddenly, I feel empowered. I lean down so that our

noses are nearly touching as I roll my hips. "Better?" I ask with a feigned look of innocence.

"Fuck, baby. When did the student become the teacher?" he manages as he thrusts up to meet my punishing rhythm.

"School's out," I say with a grin. "But the assignment needs to be completed."

I hover over him, fitting my lips against his and stroking his lower lip with my tongue. His lips part and our kiss intensifies as our joined bodies move in perfect harmony. He lets me keep control as I let myself enjoy the pace and the friction being created between us.

Our movements become erratic, both of us focused on our needs. When his hand reaches between us and his finger flicks over my sensitive nub, I feel my mouth fall open as an intense orgasm rips through me. I feel him jerk inside me before his own body tenses, a groan slipping from his lungs as he follows me over the edge.

At some point in my post-orgasmic bliss, after Emmett's taken care of the used condom and returned to bed and I lie on top of his warm body, I'm silent in my thoughts as I realize we need to have the break-up talk. To discuss the mechanics of everything, even though I really don't want to. Regardless, it was our plan and we need to carry it out. Although all the reasons why are starting to get a bit foggy.

"What's wrong?" Emmett's hand had been absentmindedly stroking my back but stops when he asks the question.

I swallow down my nerves. This has always been the endgame. Why am I so unsure about it all of a sudden?

I roll off him and sit up, leaning my back against the headboard. He mimics my move and situates himself next to me, mirroring my body's position, entwining his fingers through mine.

"We should discuss...you know..." I shrug, hesitating to go any further because I'm suddenly a big chicken shit who can't form complete sentences.

"What?" he asks.

"Our...you know...breakup," I stammer as I feel my anxiety increase. Why am I so nervous to fake break up?

"Oh," he replies quietly, his body tensing next to me as he removes his hand from mine. I feel the loss acutely as I glance over at him and see hurt in his eyes before he quickly averts his gaze.

"I mean...you're still good with us breaking up on this trip, right?" I ask, a big part of me silently hoping he'll say, "No."

I've come to realize how much I like Emmett. It's confusing to like both Hendy and Emmett. They are so different. I frown to myself as I consider why I still want to be with Hendy. Would I like Emmett this much if we were a real couple in a real relationship? Maybe sleeping with him was a bad idea and has clouded my judgment, obscuring the original goals I set.

He swallows and I watch his Adam's apple bob. "Of course."

He pauses and presses his lips together as if to keep himself from saying more.

"What? Should we do something different?" I ask hopefully. Please say you like me as much as I like you, I silently beg. Tell me we should keep going, but this time for real.

Emmett swings his legs over the side of the bed and turns his back to me when he speaks. "No. This is what we planned to do, so we should. I...I think we should have our fight over me not being able to attend that holiday party you mentioned the other day. You can say something about how you do everything for me and I don't reciprocate and do stuff for you."

"Okay," I agree hesitantly.

Emmett peers at me over his shoulder before he stands and slips on his boxer briefs.

"We might as well get it over with now. That way you can spend time with Hendy this weekend."

His words sting more than I thought they would, and anger begins to bubble up in my chest. I tug at the sheet to cover my body, feeling overexposed and vulnerable.

Do I mean so little to him that he doesn't even want to have one last night together?

"Fine, yeah," I mutter, trying to keep the hot tears that have welled up in my eyes from spilling over. I will not be *that* girl.

He hastily begins to dress with more force than necessary as I remain in bed, afraid to make a move, knowing this will be the last time we're together.

"Let's get this over with," he says, nodding toward me with a determined look on his face. "Get dressed and meet me in the kitchen in five."

He walks to the door and then pauses for a second, giving me hope he'll change his mind, but then opens it and walks out, leaving me alone and hurt.

I push the heartbreak aside and focus on the anger instead. He wants an epic fight? Well, great. He's about to get one.

* * *

"You're being a selfish bitch!" Emmett yells at me from across the kitchen island. We've been fighting for five minutes and anyone in a five-mile vicinity can hear us. I didn't think our fake breakup would feel so real.

He could have just as well slapped me in the face for how painful his words are as they slice a hole in my heart. Tears stream down my cheeks. "Fuck you, Emmett. If anyone knows about being selfish, it's you," I manage, pointing at him accusingly.

"I can't do this anymore. This," he says, motioning between us, "is over."

"Fine. Whatever," I reply as I turn on my heels and hightail it out of the kitchen. I make it out the front door onto the screened-in porch and straight into a warm wall of human.

"Hey," Hendy says in a low voice, "Are you okay?"

I open my mouth to say something but no words come out. The only noise I make is a sob.

"Come here, Luce. I got you," Hendy practically coos as he pulls me into an embrace, wrapping his arms tightly around me. "Let it all out. It'll all work out."

I cry into his chest. I should be ecstatic right now. I'm literally being held by my crush since forever. Joel Henderson is *holding* me. This was my goal. It's all I've wanted for years.

But why does it feel... all wrong?

My tears begin to dry up, my eyes too swollen to produce anymore.

"Come on. Let's get you a drink. You can sleep in my room tonight," Hendy offers.

I step back abruptly. His room? Emmett and I haven't even been broken up for five minutes and he's already invited me into his bedroom?

He puts his hands up in a defensive posture as if

reading my mind. "There's a sofa in the sitting room of the master suite. I can sleep there. You can have the bed."

"Oh," I manage as I rub my eyes. "Are you sure?"

"Of course, beautiful." He puts his hand out and I accept it. "Let's go get your things."

I follow Hendy into the house and down the back hallway. Emmett has somehow disappeared and is nowhere to be seen. I quickly pack my things and Hendy slings my bag over his shoulder, tugging me down the hall toward his bedroom. I feel strange about sharing a room with him. I'm sure I could find another space to sleep.

Emmett was being such an ass and jumped straight into action so quickly that we didn't discuss what would happen with our room. Why do I care? Angry hot tears well up again, but I manage to stop them before Hendy turns around. He drops my bag on the bed and spins in a circle with his hands out.

"Mi casa es su casa," he says with a wink.

"Well, I appreciate it," I say as I bite my lip nervously. I'm already wearing sweatpants and a T-shirt, so I grab my toothbrush and step into the bathroom. Holy shit! I'm momentarily distracted from my anger and sadness as I take in the largest shower I've ever seen. I thought the one in our room...nope, not going there. I will not allow myself to think of the orgasmic shower make-out session I just had less than an hour ago with my now ex-fake boyfriend.

I quickly brush my teeth and then head straight into an Alaskan king-sized bed, one that's so high it comes with step stools to get up into it.

"You good over there?" Hendy calls out from the adjoining space. I glance toward him. I can see his feet on the sofa, but the rest of him is hidden behind the wall separating the two rooms.

"Yeah. Thanks, Hendy," I say. "For being someone I can lean on."

"Of course. I got your back," he says. "Let me know if you need to talk about it."

I frown. Shouldn't he have Emmett's back?

I decide to just accept his hospitality and do what I can to enjoy the last day of the trip. I knew breaking up on this trip was always part of our plan, but I never thought it would hurt this much.

Maybe we should have waited until tomorrow? Now I'm stuck up here and the only person I wanted to hang out with this weekend doesn't want to be with me.

This whole fake boyfriend thing might have been the worst idea in the history of bad ideas.

Chapter Twenty-Three

E mmett

Goddammit, why does it feel like I've been hit in the chest and tackled by a two-hundred-and-fifteen-pound linebacker?

Well, besides the fact that I was just literally pushed out of bounds off the field by the opposing left tackle from the Jackson U Lumberjacks.

Today is our last official game of the season before we head into the conference championships. To say my head is not in the game is an understatement.

Since the fake fight, which didn't feel fake at all, and then coming back home from the ski trip last Sunday, I haven't seen or spoken to Lucy. After all hell broke loose between us, I saw her immediately being consoled by Hendy like she was some injured bird.

I should have done something then and there, made it

right, but that's not what Lucy wanted. We had agreed we would break up on that trip. Our ruse was up and she won her coveted prize.

I don't know what changed for me during our weekend together, but all I can think about since has been one thing: what the fuck happened between Lucy and me?

I packed my bags and left the house as soon as I saw Hendy escort Lucy down the hallway and into his room. Jesus, did he swoop in fast. I guess there's no such thing as bro code after all.

Not that I can be too mad at Hendy because he did exactly what he typically does. He goes after the girl he wants. But in this case that girl had been mine.

I'd tried to push away and bury those feelings in preparation for this final game, to ignore the anger and frustration brewing inside me this entire week.

But then, on top of all of that, I had shit go down between my dad, me, and my grandma.

My dad decided that he was going to take over all the financial matters for my grandmother and did so behind my back. Had I not been over at my grandma's house and seen the paperwork laying out on her kitchen table, I would have never been able to step in to prevent it from happening.

My dad is a mooch and would take her for every dime if he could. And because he's her son, my grandmother would do anything for him, even if it meant giving up her place to live and all her money. Thankfully, I was able to stop it before it happened. I called my dad and read him the riot act, telling him if he ever tried to do anything like this to her again, I'd get a lawyer.

He called me every name in the book, even going so far as to tell me I was dead to him and he'd never wanted me in the first place.

I'll admit that one kind of hurt.

And since then I've been nothing short of a mother-fucking monster to everyone: Hendy, Killian, my other teammates, even Nana. I know not one of them deserves my wrath, but that hasn't stopped me from being an absolute asshole to everyone.

I should have saved all of that frustration for today's game, taking it out on the field instead of those I care about. That plan may have backfired, though, and I may have gotten a little out of control after I was pushed out-of-bounds by the opposing player. I pushed back and got in his face, nearly starting a team fight. In response, the ref called a personal foul on me and we just lost fifteen yards.

Now we're at fourth and goal, I'm on the bench, and my move could potentially lose us this game.

Great.

Another reason for people to hate me and for me to hate myself this week.

From my spot on the bench, I take a sweeping glance into the crowd and toward the student section, scanning every face visible to see if there's a possibility that Lucy is here watching the game.

And then realization hits me hard. Even if she is in the stands, she's not here to see me play. She's cheering on Hendy.

The thought of the two of them together has my anger rising all over again. I throw my helmet down on the ground and let out a loud grunt, narrowly missing the equipment guy who comes to pick it up. He gives me a skeptical look before darting off, and I slam my palm down on the bench next to Killian.

Killer turns to look at me, raising an eyebrow. "Dude,

what's got your undies in a bunch? We're up by three, no need to go ballistic."

I shake my head before bending over and placing my chin in my hands, elbows digging into the pads of my thighs.

"I know...fuck, I know." I squeeze my eyes shut, trying to get Lucy out of my head and reset my state of mind. "Things are just fucked up right now."

Killer pats me on the back as the water guy hands me my water bottle. I accept it and slam back the entire contents before tossing it behind me.

"Well, there's nothing you can do about it now, so let's just focus on the game and then tonight we can go party and you can forget all about your problems."

I twist my neck to glare at him and he's grinning like a fool.

"You think that's the answer to everything? Girls and booze?"

He shrugs. "Works for me every time."

Our attention is brought back to the game as Spider, our kicker, sets up for our last attempt at a field goal before the clock runs out. The crowd goes wild as he kicks and scores the three points. Hendy appears out of the corner of my eye, congratulating everyone down the line. When he stops in front of Killer and me, he clasps us on the shoulders simultaneously, bringing in his head near ours as he yells out in celebration.

"We did it boys! Tonight, it's time to party!"

Killer gives a hoot of excitement as the bench erupts in a celebratory fashion. The band plays our school fight song and the crowd in the stands cheer along with us.

I want to be happy about this win because it's what we worked for all year long. To get to this spot, put CFU on the map when it comes to our football program. Plus, it gives me satisfaction knowing we're ending the season in a good place. Next year, my senior year, is going to be great for our football team.

Yet my heart doesn't feel that same kick of excitement like it should.

We're back in the locker room to shower, change, and celebrate our team win, a towel-wearing Hendy walks up to where I'm sitting on the bench with a serious look on his face.

"Hey, EJ, can I talk to you for a second?" he asks, almost nervously, sliding his hand through his wet hair. It's a move he often does when he's anxious about something.

"Yeah, what is it?"

"Well, I was wondering if it'd be okay with you if I asked Lucy to come with me to the party tonight?"

Fuck.

Hendy and I go way back. We've been friends since the beginning of our freshman year. We're teammates. He's our captain and my housemate. But right now, at this moment, he's my rival and I want to smash his nose in with my knuckles.

But I don't. Instead, I ball my hands into fists because this is exactly what I promised Lucy would happen.

She deserves to get the guy she wants, even if it isn't me.

I avert my gaze and throw a hand in the air, searching for my T-shirt before sliding it on over my head and arms. I need to be dressed for this conversation.

When my gaze lands back on Hendy, I can see that his normal posturing isn't there. He actually seems serious about this. But is it because he doesn't want to ruin our friendship or because he really likes Lucy?

If I'm going to give him the okay, I'm also going to set the record straight and make sure he treats her right.

"Lucy is a great girl. Just because it didn't work out with us doesn't mean that I don't care about her...*a lot*." I glare at him hard, poking him in the chest to emphasize my truth. "So if you go out with her, make damn sure you don't fuck this up. She's not like the other girls you hook up with. You feel me?"

Hendy nods his head emphatically, his eyebrows pinching inward. "Yeah, man, of course. But just say the word if you don't want me to. I respect bro code and all."

Well shit on a stick.

Here's my chance to set the record straight and tell him to fuck off because I don't want him anywhere near Lucy. To tell him that I want another chance with Lucy, this time for real. That he would be in the way of that effort.

But I can't.

This was her choice and what she wanted, what she signed up for from the very beginning, and I have to respect her wishes.

Even if it's not at all what I want.

Chapter Twenty-Four

L ucy

There's a text message on my phone when I pull it out from my bag. Since freshman year, I've worked two afternoons a week at an indie bookstore just off campus. It's an easy job and I also get twenty-five percent off books, which means I can finagle Gail, the bookstore owner, into ordering any actual physical books I've needed for classes at a super high discount. But mostly, I just love the smell of the books. It's my happy place.

> Emmett: I heard u r coming to the party tonight. Just be careful with Hendy. He's a good guy, but still a player.

I roll my eyes. Why do I feel like Emmett is just trying to sabotage my chances with Hendy? Of course, I know

Hendy is a player. If that had bothered me, then I wouldn't have agreed to our fake relationship in the first place.

I decide not to reply. I don't have time for this.

I sling my bag over my shoulder and yell my goodbye to Gail as I walk the three blocks back to my dorm. Gracie and Kelsie are both vying for the coveted position at the sink, where the lighting is best to apply their make-up and do their hair.

"Hello, ladies," I say as I drop my bag on the floor and reach in my drawer to pull out a pair of slim-fitting jeans, boots, and an off-the-shoulder, cream sweater. I grab a quick shower and get dressed, sliding past my friends who are finishing their make-up routines. The party started an hour ago, but I promised Gail I'd work till close and she stays open late on Saturdays during the holiday season.

I unravel my hair from the braids I've worn all day and run my fingers through the long waves that cascade softly down my back. I apply a little mascara, eyeliner, and colored lip balm. Stepping back, I take a quick look at myself in the mirror over my dresser.

Gracie whistles. "Damn, you look good." I meet her eyes in the mirror. Gracie has her sleek black hair in these adorable little braided pigtail buns and is wearing dark jeans and a black top.

Kelsie is in a short denim skirt, a plaid button-down tied high to reveal her slim waist, and some very cool cowboy boots. My friends are a million times more stylish than me.

"Thanks," I manage. "You ladies ready for the party?"

"Hell to the yeah! I think everyone is going to be there," Kelsie interjects as she steps out of the bathroom. "The football team owns this Saturday."

I chuckle. "Noted."

Kelsie surveys me from across the room. "So, are we going to talk about the big breakup yet?"

I shake my head. "Nope."

"You know you can trust us, right? Plus, you haven't grieved properly yet." Gracie frowns. "But then again, what do I know about relationships?"

The three of us laugh because Gracie has never actually been with a guy. She's dated a few times but never gets serious. We're pretty sure she's still a virgin.

I bite my lip. I hate not being forthcoming with my best friends. If I can't trust them, who can I trust? Certainly not Emmett.

"Listen...I...I am sort of meeting Hendy there tonight."

Both girls give me comical expressions, their eyes bugging out in surprise and shock.

But I continue on. "Emmett and I are on good terms. I mean, we're still in contact and all. I just want to move forward. Okay?"

Gracie purses her lips and she considers my announcement.

"Girl, you know I, of all people, know how much you've crushed on Hendy. I just want you to be careful. He's such a womanizer. I heard he is seeing Jessica Hoffman," Gracie says quietly.

She's not wrong. I know he has a reputation. And just because he wants to see me at the party doesn't mean I'm the only girl he's dating. I'm not that naive.

Kelsie rolls her eyes. "And by seeing," she uses air quotes. "We mean, he's been fucking her. Jessica just wants to fuck the entire team. And she's got backstabbing attitude. She's a bitch."

Gracie gives Kelsie a pointed look and Kelsie puts her

hands up defensively. "What? She is. I'm not slut-shaming, just stating facts."

"Look," I add to reassure them both of my intentions. "I'm aware of Jessica's reputation. I'm aware of Hendy's. I'm good. I swear."

"Okay. We just don't want you hurt by a guy who has gone through most of the sororities, the women's lacrosse team, and his freshman and sophomore English lit classes. But if he's who you want, then let's get your ass over to that party," Gracie says as she holds out her elbow. I loop my arm through it and stick my phone and ID in my back pocket.

We chat about our classes and our upcoming finals as we walk down the dark side streets toward the house. The telltale sounds of a party welcome us as we approach. When we turn the corner, I can see about two dozen people standing in the front yard.

The bass from the music inside can be heard cutting through the otherwise cold, quiet night. The three of us walk up the stairs to the front porch. A few football players sit on mismatched lawn chairs that cover either side of the porch. One has a girl in his lap, another leans his chair back against the railing. I get a few nods from them as we walk inside.

Once inside the party, the music is full blast. I hesitate for a moment, knowing that Emmett is somewhere in here and the possibility that we'll run into each other is high. The mere thought of seeing him makes my stomach clench with butterflies. Will he be with a new girl?

Why should I care? I shake my head to clear all the thoughts of my fake boyfriend and buck up.

"I'm going to find Hendy!" I yell. Gracie and Kelsie nod and I take off toward the kitchen, shoving my way through the throngs of people gyrating to some popular song that's playing. Halfway across the room, I feel arms come around my waist and I squeal.

"Gotcha!" Hendy whispers in my ear. I turn and grin up at him.

"Hey," I say loudly over the music.

"Hey," he replies, grinning. "You want to dance? Or I can get you a drink?"

"Let's dance," I reply. He reaches down and grasps my wrists, bringing them up to his broad shoulders, and I curl my fingers into them. I stare up dreamily into his dark and magnetic eyes. His gaze is intense as his big hands wrap around my waist, drawing me in closer. We move to the song and suddenly it feels like the room disappears.

This is what I've wanted for years. I'm here, with Joel Henderson, and I should be the happiest I've ever been, but my mind keeps replaying memories with Emmett.

Hendy slowly leans down and I know what's about to happen. I should be over the moon about it. His lips pause just before reaching mine as if seeking permission.

Fuck it. Maybe kissing Hendy will officially help me get over whatever I felt toward Emmett. I press my lips to his. His kiss isn't as gentle as Emmett's. He's a good kisser, don't get me wrong. Maybe too good, as if he's done this a thousand times before.

Hendy is suddenly yanked back, and all my thoughts vanish. I open my eyes and look up to find a furious-looking Emmett clutching Hendy's shirt.

"What the fuck, EJ?" Hendy yells as he pushes Emmett back. "You said you were cool with this."

I feel like I've been slapped in the face when I look at Emmett. He quickly glances toward me. I go from shocked to livid in two seconds.

"I literally just saw you with Jessica earlier. Remember what I said?" Emmett yells out as a small crowd starts to form around us. I look past them and see Jessica Hoffman standing in the corner. She has an angry scowl on her face and she stares me down, firing daggers at me real enough to make me bleed.

Hendy leans in and says something to Emmett, but I don't bother waiting around to listen. What the hell is happening? Hendy reaches out as I shove past him.

He leans down. "It's not what you think, Lucy. I'll explain it if you just wait."

"There's nothing to explain, Hendy. You broke your word to me."

Emmett steps between me and Hendy and takes a swing at Hendy while I head toward the door. I'm over this scene. Jessica steps in front of me as I reach the front entrance.

"Hendy's mine," she says, her fake eyelashes getting in the way as she glares at me.

I roll my eyes. "I hardly think Hendy's owned by any woman."

"Stay away from him," she practically growls at me.

"You can have him. I don't need this kind of drama," I manage to say with confidence as I push past her to the door. I quickly scan the room but don't see Gracie or Kelsie. I'll text them later. I just need to get the hell out of here.

Making my way down the stairs and through the front yard, I glance back once at the house once I reach the sidewalk, contemplating whether to go back in to let Hendy explain and give Emmett a piece of my mind. Thinking better of it, I decide to leave so I can clear my head in peace.

Parties suck. Guys suck.

Maybe I should stick with studying. I'm way better at that than this whole dating thing.

Yet I can't help feeling hurt as I walk back to my dorm room alone. Why does my heart feel this way? Why do I still want Emmett to call me and tell me he's sorry?

I don't let myself answer that because I think I'm afraid of what the truth is.

Chapter Twenty-Five

E mmett

"Dude, will you please stop with the fucking pacing? You're making me nauseous. And I'm still feeling like shit after last night."

I stop in my tracks. I've been wearing a path through our carpet, walking back and forth for the last ten minutes, but now stare at Killian, who is lounging on his bed with his phone in his hand. He does look a little green but nothing I haven't seen before. That guy bounces back like nobody's business.

"What do you care?" I ask, rolling my eyes with irritation. "You're just on your phone trying to find someone to bang."

Killian gives me his side smirk and lifts a brow, wiggling his phone at me. "Hah, that's where you're wrong. I've already got one locked down for tonight. Now I'm checking out the internship opportunities for next semester. I assume you're worried about what went down with Lucy and Hendy and not about your internship placement?"

I lift my shoulder, my mouth tightening in a stern line. "Yeah, that's another thing to add to my growing list of fuck-ups. Not only do I think I fucked up both friendships, but I don't think I want to go into the world of sports com. God, what a mess I've made of my life."

Killian swings his legs over the edge of his bed, setting his phone down next to him as he leans forward and places his forearms on his thighs.

"Bro, there is no mess that you can't get out of," he says. Then his chin pops up, eyes narrowing. "Well, unless you decide to kill somebody and end up going to jail. That might be different."

I give him a look that says, *what the hell, dude?*

"I'm not going to kill anybody! Jesus, I think you've been watching too many true crime shows." I sit down at the edge of my bed and mirror Killian's position, contemplating the choices I've made and where I want to go.

After taking a deep breath, I let it out and close my eyes. "I haven't applied for any of the internships because I'm confused. I think I might want to go into law and become an agent."

This seems to impress Killian, who lets out a vocal form of appreciation. "I could totally see that, bro. And damn, if I were going pro, I'd want you as my agent."

It's something I've been thinking about for the last semester. But then I think about all the stuff going on with Nana and my dad and just school in general, and I push those thoughts to the side. Now, as my senior year looms ahead of me, I think I want to make some changes, go in a different direction. I just don't know what that means and how I'd even be able to afford law school if that's what I need to do for that dream to come true.

I had the epiphany while on our ski trip and I wanted to share it with Lucy then, but it would have required me to share my insecurities over whether I'm smart enough to do it. And then everything else went down and those thoughts were kicked to the curb.

I had hoped to at least continue my friendship with Lucy, but after what went down last night and my ridiculous behavior, I'm not sure she'll forgive me. Or ever talk to me again.

Hendy wasn't exactly happy with me calling him out in front of everyone and being a dick toward him, but as usual, he shrugged it off like it was no big thing. I think he ended up spending the rest of the party with Jessica anyway.

Hendy is still one of my best friends, but I hate how he goes through girls like pieces of candy from a bowl, even if they are all okay with it. It wasn't fair of me to attack him like that, though, because I'm pretty sure Lucy understands that about him too.

Which is why it hurt when she chose him over me.

I thought we had a good thing going. I thought she liked me as much as I liked her.

Now I guess I need to let that go, move on, and focus on what's in my control. Which is adding a double major. I should have enough classes to meet the requirements if I can take a few more over the summer before I check out law schools.

Holy shit. I might go to law school. The thought twists my stomach in a jumble of excitement and nerves.

There's a knock on our room door and we both turn to find Hendy standing in the doorway. He has the decency to look apologetic.

"Hey guys," he says, his hands stuffed in the pockets of his jeans. He glances up, snagging me with a look of remorse and presses his lips together in a thin line. "EJ, you got a second?"

Killer makes a sound from his throat and jumps off the bed. "I need to take a shit, I'll be back in a bit." He guffaws loudly, smacking me on the back of my shoulders as he passes. "That rhymes, dudes. I'm a poet and didn't know it!"

Then he bumps his fist against Hendy's arm on the way out of the room, his cackles still heard when he closes the bathroom door.

I nod toward the bed but Hendy shakes his head. "Nah, bro, this should be quick. I just wanted to say I'm sorry for being such a dickweed last night. I was drunk and feeling overly cocky and I shouldn't have pursued Lucy. Not after you guys were together. That was a dick move and I'm sorry."

I grunt, sounding pissy. "Yeah, it kind of was, bro. But then again, I didn't tell you she was off-limits. I mean, it's not up to me who she wants to date, it's up to her...I knew I was always her second choice, which is why I think I got so angry. I'm sorry, too."

"It's fine," he says, lifting his hands in the air to show indifference. "I can tell you really liked her and I'm sorry for getting in the middle of things. I hope I'm not the reason you guys broke up."

If only he knew...

Technically, Hendy did break us up and is the reason we're not together. But I knew all along that would happen in the end. Back at the beginning, it wasn't a big deal.

I realize now...too late... that I don't want Hendy to be with Lucy.

I want to be with her.

I still want her friendship and her laughter. I still want the way she chews on her bottom lip when she's focused while studying. I still want the way she reprimands me with her cute little tutor demands when I haven't finished an assignment. I still want the way she looks—so carefree and wild—when I make her come.

Ah shit, I think I'm in love with Lucy.

I shake my head. "No, it wasn't you or what you did. It was all me."

Hendy rubs the scruff on his chin as if considering something. "Well, you know I'm not the one to give advice on relationships or anything, bro, but maybe you should go do something about that."

I give him a look. What the hell is he talking about?

"Do something about what?"

He laughs, thumping my chest with his palm. "About getting her back, you idiot."

"Lucy doesn't want to be with me. She never has," I admit, clamming up just before I start explaining the deal that Lucy and I had agreed on. I guess she wouldn't want me telling anyone about our fake relationship. And honestly, I'd like to keep that under wraps too.

"Dude, I think you're blind. She was totally watching you the entire time we were dancing together. It's you she wants, not me. But you have to get your head out of your ass first and go talk to her."

I don't think Hendy is right about his assessment—it's not like he has any clue about our relationship background —but there is only one way to find out. And that's to act on his advice and go talk to her.

"Yeah, maybe you're right, bruh. I guess it wouldn't hurt to figure out where things stand."

Hendy slaps me on the shoulder like he's congratulating us both on a big win.

"Okay, then my work here is done." He smiles broadly and I can't help but smile back. Hendy's Romeo ways sometimes get in the way of who he truly is. He's not as bad as people think.

Just as Hendy turns toward the door, Killian pops his head back in, making a sound of relief and with a cheesy smile on his face.

"Are we done here?" he asks, his eyes snapping between both of us. "Cuz I think it's time to feed the Killer beast and drink some beer." He pats his stomach and nods his head enthusiastically like a golden retriever.

"I could go for some food," Hendy replies. "You coming with us, EJ?"

I heave a sigh of exasperation, running a hand through my hair. "No thanks...I can't. It's Sunday and I need to go see my grandma. You guys have fun."

And then I give Killian a knowing look, pointing at him with my index finger in accusation.

"Do not," I say with authority, "I repeat, do not get extra jalapeños and onions on your burger this time. You stunk up the room for days the last time, bro."

Killian laughs hard and gives me an innocent look. "I lit some girly candles. It wasn't that bad."

"Dude, you work with farm animals in a barn. Of course you didn't think it was bad!"

Killian gives me the finger and walks off, leaving me with the last word when he says, "*Mooooo.*"

Chapter Twenty-Six

L ucy

I stare at the freshman sitting across from me. My professor asked me to help her so she could pass her upcoming finals. I was wrong when I thought Emmett was a lost cause because she takes the cake.

"Emily, let's just pick it up from here on Tuesday. Try to go through the handouts I gave you and we can work from there during our next session," I say, packing up my bag and doing my best to keep the frustration out of my voice.

She gives me a meager smile and hurries to get her things. I watch her race out of the library and into the arms of some guy who waits for her out on the front steps. They hug and kiss and a zing of envy shoots through me.

I'm not sure if it's because I want that too, a guy waiting for me to run into his arms, telling me how much he's missed me, even if it's only been a few hours. The confusing part is I don't know if I want that kind of love and affection from Hendy or Emmett.

GAH. I'm so confused.

I haven't spoken to either of them since the night of the party. Hendy texted me an apology, but it seemed half-assed. Emmett hasn't tried to contact me at all.

Oddly, I'm more upset about Emmett, which makes no sense.

My phone pings and I look down to see a message from Gracie.

> Gracie: Uh...are you still sort of with Hendy?

I frown as I try to figure out why she's asking.

> Me: Probably not. I don't think so. Maybe?

I head out of the library and start walking toward the dorms.

> Gracie: Oh. Okay.

> Me: Why?

> Gracie: Well, I just saw Jessica kissing Hendy outside that bar down the street from Culver Hall.

I don't reply. Instead, I change course and head in that direction, feeling a strange array of emotions. Part of me is angry at Jessica because she was so rude to me and is clearly trying to mark Hendy as hers and hers alone. I'm also annoyed at Hendy and his cavalier attitude.

But mostly I'm mad at myself for putting him on a pedestal all these years. I should have put myself on that pedestal instead. I want more than just being a fling at a party and I'm worthy of more.

I shrug off those feelings when another wave of emotion hits me.

I'm hurt over how things are between Emmett and me. Hell, I'm confused why I still care about Emmett.

Without another thought as to what I'm doing and why, I march straight toward the college bar down a side street behind a few university buildings. Just as I get to the entrance, Hendy opens the door and he and Jessica walk outside.

I stop in my tracks, oddly feeling nothing. The anger has subsided. I'm annoyed and my pride is a little bruised, but that's it. I swallow as realization hits me like a sucker punch to the face.

I love Emmett. I've been in love with Emmett for weeks now.

Oh shit.

How did I not see that? I was so busy being hyper-focused on winning Hendy's attention that I completely missed the fact that I'd given my heart to someone else. I was so goal-oriented that I couldn't see the trees through the forest.

God, I'm a total idiot. I had the perfect guy... and I blew it.

And what's worse, I blew it over a guy that I didn't really want. I mean, I wanted the idea of Joel Henderson. I wanted that made-up high school popularity moment that I craved years ago. But now...I just want Emmett.

Hendy stops abruptly, throwing an arm around Jessica

as they approach me. Jessica's gaze follows his and she smirks.

"Hi, Lucy," she says, her voice sweet. Too sweet. The kind of sweetness that has daggers hidden underneath.

"Hey," I reply, not giving her a second glance. Then my attention turns to Hendy. "Hendy, uh, do you have two seconds?"

Hendy peers down at Jessica and back to me before nodding. He glances over my shoulder at another football player who's walking out with his girlfriend.

"Jess, go ask K-man and Olive if they want to come over for the pre-exams barbecue next weekend," he says to Jessica.

She stares at him for a beat and then at me and I can see the struggle written all over her face. She doesn't want to lose him to another girl.

"I'll just be a minute," I assure her. "You can have him right back. I promise."

Her features morph into a look of confusion as if she isn't sure she can trust me, but what I said was definitely not what she expected.

"Yeah, sure," she mutters as she leans up on her toes to plant a kiss on his cheek before she runs to catch up with their friends.

Hendy shifts on his feet, clearly uncomfortable.

"Listen," I start, "I..." I trail off suddenly, not sure where to begin.

Hendy gives me a small smile. "You like Emmett," he states.

I feel my eyebrows shoot skyward. I swallow. "Yeah," I manage to squeak out. It reminds me of the time when Emmett called me out on liking Hendy. Am I that easy to read? I guess it's a good thing that I never took a theater class because apparently, I suck at acting.

He chuckles and puts a hand on my shoulder, giving it a squeeze. "I'm sorry about the other night. I...I'm an idiot. I was an idiot in high school for not seeing how amazing you are and I'm an idiot now for...well, I'm an idiot, let's just leave it at that."

I try to fight the grin, but it breaks through anyhow. I shrug in agreement. "Maybe a little bit."

He nods. "You deserve to be happy. You're a good person, Lucy. And I'm...well, the jury is still out about me. But you know who is also a good person?"

"Emmett," I state softly. "Do you by chance know where he is right now?"

Nodding, he releases his hand from my shoulder and sticks it in his pocket. "He's at his grandmother's house. It's not something he talks about a lot. But he's over there most Sunday nights."

"Huh?" I ask, surprised. "His grandma? He's there a lot?" I start to put a few puzzle pieces together. Is that where he sneaks off to? Why he was late so often or didn't show up for our study sessions? Why wouldn't he tell me about her?

"Yeah. I don't know a lot about the situation, but I think he helps her way more than he lets on. Anyhow, I should probably go," he says as he motions in the direction Jessica went.

"Hendy?" I ask as he pauses, peering back over his shoulder toward me.

"You're a good guy, too." I smirk. "Don't worry, I won't tell anyone."

He laughs and turns back to me, wrapping his big arms around my shoulders and pulls me into a hug. I wrap my arms around his waist and hug him back. He kisses the top of my head.

"Just know, Lucy-goosey, you're in the inner circle now, so if you ever need anything, just ask."

"Thanks, Hendy. Same. Now, you better get going, Jessica seems ready to claw our eyes out."

He presses his lips together as the corners of his mouth twitch. "Yeah, she's quite the wild cat in and out of the... well, you know."

I shake my head and cover my eyes with my hand. "TMI. I'll see you later."

I'm about to leave when I realize I have no idea where to find Emmett's grandmother's house. I turn around and glance at Hendy. "Wait, where..."

He raises a knowing eyebrow and gives me a crooked smile.

"Her house is the blue one with the white shutters on the second block of Elm Street."

I furrow my brows.

"Emmett's grandmother's house," he replies without prompt. "He doesn't know that I know that, but Killer pointed it out to me once. You should hurry, though. It looks like it could pour any second now."

The skies that were a light cloudy gray earlier today suddenly darken and I start walking faster, turning the corner, and nearly sprinting toward Elm Street. By the time I reach the block, rain drops fall on my head and I shiver as cold rain begins to pelt my hair and runs down my face.

I begin to jog, crossing over to the other side of the street before I slow. Emmett is out in front of a small blue bungalow with a dark red front door, using a shovel to dig up something in the yard. Is he gardening? I can't tell from where I am.

When I reach the edge of the yard, I come to a stop, covertly watching him for a solid ten seconds as the rain now pours down in sheets. He's wearing a long-sleeved blue T-shirt and dark gray sweatpants that are drenched and clinging to every single muscle I've become acquainted with over the past few weeks.

The world around me seems to stop. The water droplets on metal cars and roofs create a musical symphony of pings and splatters. I'm getting drenched even with my jacket on, but I don't care. I just need a minute to compose myself before I get his attention.

Only the universe has different ideas because out of the blue, Emmett turns and finds me staring at him.

He drops the shovel and says something, but I can't hear him over the loud soundtrack of the rain.

"What?" I call out.

He speaks again, cupping his hands around his mouth. "What are you doing here?"

"I..." I can't form the words, staring blindly around because I have no idea what to say.

My brain goes blank as I start to run toward him, picking up speed as he opens his arms at the last second. I jump into them. My feet leave the ground as our lips crash together. Our clothes are drenched, and we're both shivering, but I don't care because I'm right where I should be, in Emmett's arms.

I'm not sure if it's a minute or an eternity that we kiss, but when we both pull back to breathe, his eyes are locked with mine. Bravery like I've never felt before permeates every cell in my body.

"I love you, Emmett Hudson," I whisper.

He seems stunned for a half second and then his lips turn upward. "I love you, too, Lucy."

He kisses me again then stops suddenly as I protest until he continues, "Let's get you inside. You're freezing."

I nervously peer over at the door. "Your grandma..."

"She's sleeping right now. You can meet her later," he says as he grabs my hand and pulls me toward the door.

Inside, we both kick off our shoes and he drags me down a hallway, down a set of stairs, and into the basement where he opens a door. I'm surprised to find a bedroom with an attached bathroom.

"You lived here?" I ask, taking in what looks like a teenage boy's room. "Why didn't you ever mention this—or her—before?"

He shrugs. "My dad...well, let's just say we are not on good terms. I moved in here my junior year of high school to help my grandparents, and now just my grandma," he admits as he surveys his room. There are posters of several professional football teams and a few bands. A black light sits on top of a dresser and a few airplanes made of Lego sit on a shelf alongside sci-fi books and some comic books.

He shuts the door and steps toward me, palming my cheeks. "I'm sorry I didn't tell you. I guess I was embarrassed because I have such a dysfunctional family. I was just trying to keep my college life and family priorities separate."

Well, shit, there's a lot of apologies occurring today.

"I'm sorry, too," I say.

He frowns. "You have nothing to be sorry about, Lucy. You're perfect. We were perfect and I fucked that up. I should have never let you go."

My eyes well with tears. He brushes one away as it runs down my cheek. I shiver.

"Let's get out of these wet clothes and warmed up," he says as he whips his shirt off. I gaze at the beauty that is Emmett's body as he chucks off his socks, underwear, and sweatpants, then start taking off my jacket and soaked jeans. When we're both naked, he takes my hand and pulls me into his bathroom, turning on the shower and cranking it to hot.

He helps me inside, following behind me and shutting the glass door. He puts a hand on the wall on either side of me.

"Lucy...I fucked up. But I won't do it again. I finally know who I am when I'm with you. You've given me the confidence to know that I can have the future I want." He pauses and presses wet kisses along my collarbone. I groan. "Because of you, I know what I want to do with my life."

I reach up to touch his cheek. "Really?"

He nods. "I'm going to apply to law school. I didn't think I could do that. But you didn't just tutor me. You showed me I'm capable of so much more."

"Wow, that's amazing, Emmett. I'm so proud of you. You're going to be a great lawyer. And you are capable of anything you set your mind to," I say, stroking my hand over the short beard covering his jawline.

"Agent. I want to be a sports agent."

"You'll be amazing at it," I reply, letting my hand trail down his pectoral muscles and over his washboard abs. I take his erection in my hand, and he groans.

"Fuck, Lucy. I've missed you."

"The student becomes the teacher," I state with a saucy smirk.

"Fuck, yeah you did," he manages as his jaw clenches as I run a fingertip over the crown of his cock.

I use my other hand to motion between us. "This...isn't fake anymore, is it?"

He drops his hands to the curve of my butt and pulls me up against his body, Pressing my back against the shower wall for leverage. I wrap my legs around his waist and slowly slide down onto his erection. We both let out a sound of contentment.

"No, babe. This is not fake. I'm not sure if it ever was," he admits as I start moving against him, needing a release, needing to feel like he's all mine.

"Fuck, Lucy. Wait. We need a condom," he mutters.

"I'm on the pill," I whisper back. "And I trust you."

"Jesus, Lucy," he practically growls, his cock pressed hard and hot inside me. "I've never done it before bare. You have no idea how good you feel," he adds with another groan.

He uses one hand to steady us with my back against the wall as he slides in and out of me, his pace picking up as I feel myself climbing higher onto that precipice. "Don't stop," I urge, gripping behind his neck.

"I'll never stop, baby," he grunts as we both frantically chase our releases. He presses his mouth to mine, catching my scream as I tip over the edge into the abyss of pleasure that awaits me.

I feel him twitch and still as he empties his release inside me. And then silence follows, the only noise the shower water hitting the tiles and our breaths comingling.

He drops his head and touches his forehead to mine. "I've never been happier to have needed a tutor in my life."

"I've never been happier to have had a fake boyfriend," I retort with a laugh that soon dies when I feel him grow hard again.

He thrusts his hips, moving inside me. "Does this feel fake to you?"

I shake my head.

"Good. Because from this moment forward, Lucy, we are officially back together and you're my real girlfriend. No more lying to people. This. Is. Real. You feel me?" he says, accentuating each word with a deep thrust.

"Oh, yeah." I squeeze my inner muscles around him, and he groans. "I feel you."

"This is going to be so much fun, isn't it?"

Giggling, I press a quick kiss to his lips. "So much fun."

He slowly lets me slide down his body, missing his warmth and our connection, but his arms wrap around me, and he leans down.

"I think you need a new goal, because you sure as fuck can never even look in Hendy's direction again," he says.

I laugh. "I spoke with him. It's all good."

"You talked to him?"

Nodding, I lean up to lock gazes with him once more. "And I do have a new goal."

"What's that?" His hand tries to distract me by rubbing circles on my back.

"To make love to my real, hot-as-hell, wide-receiver boyfriend."

His eyes darken. It feels like our souls are connected, like he can see straight into my mind. "Now that's a goal I can help you with."

Emmett turns off the water and we grab towels to dry off, then head back to his bedroom.

"I think I'm going to enjoy reaching this goal much more than the last one," I state.

Emmett's eyes rove over my body. "I know I am."

He leans down and kisses me, taking his time and pouring all his love into it. The towel slips free, and he presses his naked body against mine.

"Best goal ever," I whisper against his lips, savoring every taste, noise and move he makes.

None of which is faked.

Epilogue

E mmett - End of Spring Semester

"Listen up, everyone...I have an announcement!"

My gaze leaves the enormous piece of fried chicken I was just about to devour from my plate and lifts to Kelsie, Lucy's friend, who stands up from her spot on the picnic blanket where she was sitting just moments before. Everyone in the group circle stops what they're doing, all our eyes landing on Kelsie, watching and waiting as she smooths down the pleats of her floral sundress. She's by far the most dramatic and attention-grabbing out of Lucy and her friend group, IMHO.

Since finals week begins on Monday, Lucy had the idea of having a group picnic out in the quad. A last hurrah before we all dig in and stress out this weekend over studying and then go our separate ways for the summer until we return next fall.

For once I'm not worried about my finals or my tests because my head and heart have been too focused on the time I've been spending with Lucy and worried about what happens over the summer break.

My eyes bounce to Lucy, who sits next to me to see if she knows what this is about. I raise my eyebrow. In return she shrugs and gives a small quick shake of her head.

We've spent nearly every day together since that moment she showed up at my grandma's house earlier this year. She met Nana later that day and those two have since become thick as thieves. Nana wholeheartedly approves of our relationship and keeps dropping hints about future plans for weddings and babies.

We may have professed our love and commitment, but we're not quite there yet. I still have one last year of school and Lucy has two before graduating. Then there's the small task of me applying to law school and hopefully getting in. So yeah, we have a lot going for us right now, but the way I feel about her is so big that I can't imagine us not together for the long term.

It does leave the summer in question, though. I need to stay close to Grandma and work, then football practice begins in early August. Lucy plans to return home for a month to spend time with her family, whom I met over spring break, including her firefighter brother, Landon, whose glare when we first met had me wondering if he'd even rescue me if I was trapped in a burning building. I think he finally warmed up to me, but that's only because I offered him two tickets to one of our home games next season before Lucy returns to campus.

But the one thing we have decided is that when she returns for the fall semester, she'll move into the house with me, and we'll be shacking up in my bedroom.

When I first told this to Killian, he was both thrilled that he would have a room of his own once Dimitri moved out of the attic upstairs upon graduation, but also bummed that we'd no longer be roommates. We've been roommates for three years so it will be a big change for both of us. I guess that's what growing up is: learning to be thankful for the experiences and people that brought us to where we are today.

When I think back to the first time I met Lucy outside the library steps, I never would have imagined my tutor would turn into my fake girlfriend and then into my lifelong love. Go figure.

Life sure provides a lot of unexpected twists and turns.

My attention returns to Kelsie, who swings her arms wide to gather everyone's attention.

"I just got off the phone with my dad this morning who informed me that he is sending me to France for the summer to visit my aunt and then I'm spending the fall semester abroad. Isn't that so exciting?"

Lucy and Grace both squeal in delight and jump up from their spots to envelop Kelsie in a group hug. Killian snorts and continues stuffing his face with potato salad. I offer a one-handed thumbs-up, my other hand bringing the piece of chicken to my mouth.

"Oh my God, I'm so excited for you!" Lucy exclaims as she dances exuberantly in a friend-huddle dance with her besties.

I take in the scene of the three of them and immediately notice Grace's expression morphs from excitement to what looks like confusion. She steps back and tips her head to the side.

"But wait," Grace asks with a quiet timidity. "What does this mean for our living arrangement for next year?"

I don't know Grace very well, but she seems extremely smart with a big-city sophistication. From what Lucy told me, Grace grew up in San Francisco until her parents divorced and she moved with her dad, a tech millionaire, when he bought a ranch outside of the town where Lucy grew up.

Kelsie grants Grace an apologetic smile before placing her hands on top of Grace's shoulders.

"I'm sorry, Gracie. I wanted to tell you earlier, but everything all came together today. I can't pass up this opportunity. When I applied for this, Lucy was still our roommate, too. I hope you're not mad."

Something that looks like abandonment flickers over Gracie's face before it disappears, and she plasters on a smile for her friend.

Grace waves a hand in the air and pulls her friend into a tight hug as they rock back and forth together.

"Don't be silly, girl. I'm thrilled for you, Kels..."

Killian and I continue chowing on our lunches as the girls finally settle back on a blanket and continue to pepper Kelsie with questions.

So, when do you leave?

Have you been practicing your French?

Are you going to miss us?

What if you meet a guy while you're there?

And then, going in a completely different direction, Gracie lobs out the next question about her upcoming living arrangements.

"Um, you guys...this sucks! I mean, I'm happy for you both, but I won't have either one of you for roommates."

Grace's watery eyes bounce between Lucy and Kelsie, looking like a puppy who is being given up for adoption. Her chin even quivers a little bit.

Lucy reaches over and places a hand on Grace's knee. "It'll be fine, Gracie. Maybe you can apply to have your own dorm room next year."

"Yeah, you're an only child. You should be ecstatic to get your own space back to yourself," Kelsie chirps, stealing a brownie from Lucy's plate. Lucy gives a small growl and smacks her friend's hand away but she's not quick enough. Kelsie grins proudly as she bites into the chocolate dessert.

None of this seems to appease Grace as she stares down at her plate, picking at the food on it before lifting a grape to her mouth, then popping it inside and swallowing.

Killian—who's been quiet for the most part, chomping away at his food—suddenly pipes in with his very surprising suggestion.

"Well, there's always room up in the attic with me."

The entire group falls silent, our wide-eyed gazes plastered on Killian. When he looks up, he finds us all staring at him.

"What?" he asks innocently, sounding an awful lot like Chandler Bing from *Friends*. "The attic is the size of an entire floor. There's plenty of room for all your clothes and shoes and whatnot, Grace."

Laughter ensues and the conversation swiftly moves to other important matters...like the end-of-year bash being held at one of the frat houses. Leaving all the uncertainty behind for another time.

* * *

Much later, when Lucy's naked and warm body is snuggled tightly in my arms, our bodies still slick from sex, she makes a sigh of contentment as I breathe in the fragrant scent of her shampoo.

"Next year is sure going to be different," she says rather dreamily, shifting her ass deeper into my crotch.

I nudge her a bit with my now semi-erect cock, which, although very recently sated, could always go for seconds.

I place a kiss on top of her head. My hand trails down the flat of her stomach, splaying my fingers wide over her middle.

"Yeah, it will definitely be different. But I like the idea of being able to do this every night with you and not having to worry about Killian walking in on us."

Lucy laughs. "Do you really think having our own room will stop him from barging in? He's kind of oblivious to a closed door. Was he born in a barn?"

I join her in laughter because she's right. Killian has an uncanny ability to walk in at the most inopportune times.

I prop my head up into my palm, my elbow pressed into the mattress, and I shift away some of the strands of hair falling over Lucy's face. She blinks up at me and smiles.

Staring down into her beautiful eyes, I can't believe how lucky I am. There is nothing fake about this girl or how I feel about her.

I place a kiss on top of her nose. "First thing tomorrow I'm going out to the hardware store to buy a new door handle with a lock."

Lucy giggles and I take the opportunity to tickle her in one of her ribs. She squirms to try and get away, which doesn't help in detracting the attention given to my growing erection.

Flipping her over onto her back, I straddle her hips, both hands bracketing her sides as I lean down and crush my mouth to hers, letting my tongue slide between her lips and savoring every moment with her.

Her hands move to my waist and slip down further as

she settles her palms on the curve of my ass, giving me a generous squeeze.

"I think a lock will come in very handy," she agrees, moving her legs out so I can nestle at the junction of her thighs. "Because there's still a lot I have to learn from my teacher."

My cock slides upwards through her wet folds and she gasps loudly.

"I think there's still a lot we can both teach each other. One lesson after another."

THE END

More to Read in CFU

We hope you enjoyed Book #1 in the CFU college football series! There's more to enjoy from this CFU crew, including Grace and Killer's book in Falling for the Roommate, as well as Kelsie and her Paris fling, and the forever playboy QB, Hendy.

Falling for the Roommate (Grace & Killian)
> **Falling for the Football Player** (Kelsie & Hayes)
> **Falling for the Quarterback** (Hendy and Lottie)

And if you'd like to read more books from the co-writing duo of SE Rose and Sierra Hill, check out our small-town, brothers, firefighters romance series, ***Fanning the Flames*** where Lucy Parker's brother, Landon, makes an appearance.

Now on Kindle Unlimited.
Burned
Ignited
Scorched

About the Authors

USA Today & International Bestselling romance author, **S.E. Rose** lives near Washington D.C. with her family.

When she's not wrangling her cats or keeping up with her kids, she's plotting her next story.

She loves all things wine, coffee, and cats.

In her non-existent free time, she enjoys traveling, going to concerts, binging on her favorite shows, and reading, especially if it's a good mystery or comedy.

Learn more about upcoming books from S.E. Rose at www.seroseauthor.com or follow her on Facebook and Instagram.

Sierra Hill is a ***RONE Award-Winning*** author of ***Game Changer***, as well as over 40 novels, including the college sports series, ***Courting Love***, and her latest hockey series, ***Vancouver Vikings***.

Subscribe to her email list and download a FREE book here: https://www.sierrahillbooks.com//newsletter

www.ingramcontent.com/pod-product-compliance
Lightning Source LLC
Chambersburg PA
CBHW030138010826
48973CB00002B/624